The man was slowly loosening his hold on the Colt .45 in his right hand. He was blinking rapidly and crossing his eyes slightly as he stared up, aghast, at the horn handle of the thick bowie knife protruding from the dead middle of his forehead. Blood oozed from the deep cut made by the knife blade driven into his skull and shone darkly in the morning light pushing through the saloon's front windows.

He fell straight back as though all his bones had turned to jelly, then slammed onto the table behind him with a loud, crunching thud.

Lowering his Colt, Longarm turned to rake his gaze across War Cloud to Magpie, still crouched about five feet back in the same position as when she'd whipped the savage blade out of its scabbard and sent it careening into the man's head . . .

DON'T MISS THESE ALL-ACTION WESTERN SERIES FROM THE BERKLEY PUBLISHING GROUP

THE GUNSMITH by J. R. Roberts

Clint Adams was a legend among lawmen, outlaws, and ladies. They called him . . . the Gunsmith.

LONGARM by Tabor Evans

The popular long-running series about Deputy U.S. Marshal Custis Long—his life, his loves, his fight for justice.

SLOCUM by Jake Logan

Today's longest-running action Western. John Slocum rides a deadly trail of hot blood and cold steel.

BUSHWHACKERS by B. J. Lanagan

An action-packed series by the creators of Longarm! The rousing adventures of the most brutal gang of cutthroats ever assembled—Quantrill's Raiders.

DIAMONDBACK by Guy Brewer

Dex Yancey is Diamondback, a Southern gentleman turned con man when his brother cheats him out of the family fortune. Ladies love him. Gamblers hate him. But nobody pulls one over on Dex . . .

WILDGUN by Jack Hanson

The blazing adventures of mountain man Will Barlow—from the creators of Longarm!

TEXAS TRACKER by Tom Calhoun

J.T. Law: the most relentless—and dangerous—manhunter in all Texas. Where sheriffs and posses fail, he's the best man to bring in the most vicious outlaws—for a price.Tabor Evans.

TABOR EVANS

LONGARM

AND THE WAR CLOUDS

J

JOVE BOOKS, NEW YORK

THE BERKLEY PUBLISHING GROUP
Published by the Penguin Group
Penguin Group (USA) LLC
375 Hudson Street, New York, New York 10014

USA • Canada • UK • Ireland • Australia • New Zealand • India • South Africa • China

penguin.com.

A Penguin Random House Company

LONGARM AND THE WAR CLOUDS

A Jove Book / published by arrangement with the author

For information, address: The Berkley Publishing Group,
a division of Penguin Group (USA) LLC,
375 Hudson Street, New York, New York 10014.

ISBN: 978-0-515-15380-4

PUBLISHING HISTORY
Jove mass-market edition / December 2013

PRINTED IN THE UNITED STATES OF AMERICA

10 9 8 7 6 5 4 3 2 1

Cover illustration by Milo Sinovcic.

Chapter 1

"I don't think there's anything quite as grand as a good ball—wouldn't you agree, Custis?" asked Cynthia Larimer.

"Took the words right out of my mouth, little lady," agreed the deputy U.S. marshal known far and wide by friend and foe as Longarm.

Cynthia had come up behind the federal lawman to speak into his ear as he leaned in the doorway of the ballroom in General William Larimer's sprawling, mansard-roofed mansion on Denver's high-toned Sherman Avenue.

The General was considered by most to be Denver's founding father. As impressive as the title was, Longarm admired the man more for being the uncle of Miss Cynthia Larimer, Denver's unofficial, raven-haired, blue-eyed princess. It didn't seem to matter that the twenty-three-year-old Larimer heiress, being a precocious young adventuress with many friends in high

places throughout the world, spent most of her free time elsewhere.

And, being rich, she had nothing but free time.

That included art openings in Italy, royal weddings in France, Christmases with counts and countesses in eastern Europe, antique-shopping in London, and, most recently, a celebration at the Smithsonian in Washington, D.C., for the unveiling of three dinosaurs pieced together from bones found in Maryland.

When Cynthia was in Denver, however, as she was now for the annual summer Governor's Ball hosted by "Uncle Groggy and Aunt May," as she so quaintly referred to the General and his sweet, gray-headed, slightly doddering wife, Longarm often found himself not uncomfortably locked in the ravishing beauty's gravitational pull.

Cynthia furtively brushed her hand across Longarm's hand as she stood beside him in the ballroom's broad doorway, taking in the thirty or so immaculately attired men and women dancing an energetic waltz being played by an orchestra that Cynthia herself, along with Aunt May and the governor's wife and personal secretary, had chosen from a pool of musicians spread across the country.

The young heiress said just loudly enough for Longarm to hear her above the music and hum of conversation, "I'd like to have something else in my mouth about now, Custis." She gave him a sly, sidelong glance. "And you know just what I mean."

The governor's nephew, whose name Longarm had forgotten ten seconds after he'd been introduced to the lad by the General, was standing about four feet ahead of Longarm and Cynthia, to their left. He just then

turned to frown over his shoulder at the pair. The nephew's tiny, round, gold-framed spectacles glinted in the lights of the shimmering gas jets and the massive, popping hearth.

The pale young man studied the ravishing beauty and the tall lawman with the dark brown longhorn mustache clad in a three-piece tweed suit, and then, apparently not believing his ears, smiled politely at the pair, dipped his chin, and turned his head forward again to continue enjoying the dance.

Longarm felt his cheeks warm with what he assumed was a crimson flush. When he gave Cynthia an admonishing glower, the girl merely looked up over the big lawman's shoulder and winked. She brushed her hand against his once more and rose up on her tiptoes to say huskily into his ear, "Why don't you bribe one of the cab drivers into meeting me at the buggy shed door in a half hour. I'll fetch my cape and freshen up and meet you there."

"Cynthia, I'm not sure this is the night for . . ."

"I'll be leaving for New York the day after tomorrow, Custis," she said, beetling her black brows and pooching out her pink lips in a pout. "And since you'll be back to work tomorrow, off on another one of your risky assignments, one of which is bound to get you killed one of these days, we won't see each other again in months. If ever. Maybe not till Christmas, at the earliest."

She leaned closer against him until their shoulders touched. "I really, really want to have one last night . . . alone . . . with *you, Custis.* Don't you want to have one night alone with *me*?"

"Well, sure I do, but . . ."

Longarm glanced down at the girl's heaving bosom, which was all but exposed by the low-cut black dress that matched the girl's raven hair and complimented the cobalt blue of her eyes. Diamond earrings dangled to her shoulders, inside the long tresses dropping to the middle of the girl's shapely back.

Her breasts rose and fell . . . rose and fell. He thought he could see her nipples come alive behind her corset.

Longarm glanced around to make sure no one was watching him and the heiress. It would have been a faux pas on a grand scale and of epic proportions if anyone were to learn that a lowly federal employee was making time with the princess of Denver. That would have been like having a broomtail mustang run down out of the desert hills to squirt its foul seed into a Thoroughbred mare from a royal line.

Longarm and Cynthia had to be careful. If anyone should find out that Longarm was any more than her unofficial bodyguard, who occasionally accompanied the heiress to Denver operas and Christmas and Fourth of July parties, the disgrace would be so acute that the Larimer family might very well commit suicide en masse—not to mention run the lowly lawman out of town on a greased rail.

Cynthia seemed to be reading his mind. She brushed her bare shoulder against his and said while looking over the crowd, "Come on, Custis. Surely the famous lawman who runs down owlhoots of the worst stripe daily without batting an eye isn't afraid of a harmless little tryst."

"Girl, our trysts are neither harmless nor little . . ."

"That's for sure." She chuckled, turning her head away as though to peruse the sprawling lunch table and crystal punch bowl. "After the last time, I was walking bull-legged for a week!"

She turned to him, brushing the side of her bosom against his arm. "Let's go to your place."

"My place?"

"Too noisy around here."

"But how will you get back?"

"We'll have the driver wait. Surely he won't mind if he's well paid."

"Too dangerous. The driver might let the cat out of the bag."

"Cab drivers are good at keeping secrets. Especially . . ."

"Yeah, I know," Longarm growled, smiling at an elderly lady meeting his gaze from several feet to his right. "Especially if they're well paid. All right, if we're going to do this, let's do it." Just the idea of frolicking with the comely heiress was causing his shorts to grow tight across his crotch.

"I'll inform Aunt May that I'm having one of my headaches and am heading for bed." She rubbed her breasts against his arm again and flicked a hand across the collar of his black frock coat, as though flicking away lint.

He wished she'd stop doing that before his lust became obvious. He could feel his shorts begin to tent. Besides, he had a feeling the governor's bespectacled son was growing suspicious of the princess of Denver and the rangy, sun-browned lawman she'd invited to the ball and who was now standing rather too closely beside her.

The young man kept glancing furtively over his shoulder, though he might merely be ogling Cynthia's tits. Most every man at the ball had appraised them at least once, Longarm had noted, automatically, odiously jealous. Even the governor himself had asked Cynthia to dance more times than Longarm, who'd only danced with her once, thought proper. She was more than half the old, married fool's age, after all, and despite his station the governor had no more chance nuzzling those firm, round orbs than did an elephant over in Africa.

Longarm watched her walk away from him, admiring the natural sway of her round bottom below the long, cool, inverted V of her exposed back. The girl could make a dress come alive like none other whom Longarm had ever known. The taffeta and silk jostled and swayed in all the right places, driving men crazy with the imagined images of all it concealed.

Cynthia smiled and nodded at all who stepped aside for the ravishing, glittering, black-haired beauty as she made her way over to where Aunt May was sitting with the General, the governor, and the governor's wife. The governor saw her coming well in advance—the old fellow's eyes had probably been raking the crowd for her—and he nearly fell over in his chair when he too hastily stood too far in advance of Cynthia's arrival for his wife not to notice and give him a look.

Longarm chuckled.

When he thought enough time had passed for his own leave-taking not to look suspicious, he took it, giving the General's son, who'd glanced at him again suspiciously, a cordial dip of the chin. The lawman retrieved his hat from one of the pretty, young gals tending the

coatroom and headed through the grand foyer and outside into the porte cochere where the drivers of the hansom cabs were smoking, conversing, and sneaking sips from hide-wrapped flasks.

Fifteen minutes later, Longarm was riding up beside his old friend, Siggi Olafsson, who'd been driving hansom cabs around Denver since the railroad had come to town back in the early '70s and Denver had start growing beyond its cow town roots.

Olafsson took a swig from his own flask as he pulled his Percheron along the cinder-paved trail that formed a semicircle around the Larimer's sprawling mansion, the flickering lamplight in the windows dimming the stars over Denver and limning the tops of the trimmed hedges in fluttering gold. It was almost midnight—a balmy midsummer night with the smell of ladies' perfume wafting on a gentle breeze flowing down from the Rockies.

The music from the ballroom danced over the dew-damp grass.

"Who is it this time, Custis?" Olafsson asked.

"Wouldn't you like to know, Siggi?"

Longarm removed his sweat-soaked paper collar with a relieved sigh and tossed it onto the seat. Whoever said that grown men should wear strips of paper tight enough around their necks to look fashionable despite their bulging eyes should be drawn and quartered.

The lawman rubbed his neck, groaning luxuriously.

Olafsson extended his flask. "Have you a sip o' that, Custis. You look like you could use it."

Longarm accepted the flask and tipped it back. He brought it back down, making a face. "God, that's awful!"

"Well, it ain't your Tom Moore, I'll grant ya," the

middle-aged man said in his Norwegian brogue that wasn't quite as thick as it once was, "but it's all I can afford."

"I'll buy you a bottle of Tom Moore if you keep your mouth shut about tonight. And my . . . uh . . . *friend* will pad your pockets so you can buy a bottle or two of your own. Maybe have enough left over for the opera."

Longarm grinned at his old friend, who famously did not care for the opera though he naturally had to work the opera crowds down around Union Station and Sixteenth Street for his clientele.

Olafsson chuffed a caustic laugh. "I'd just like enough leftover to afford one of them doxies at the Black Cat. The prices have gone up over there, you know, since Shackleton started bringing in girls from Kansas City with full sets of teeth. And I hear they can sing."

"I always said teeth were highly overvalued in a woman," Longarm said, puffing one of his three-for-a-nickel cheroots. He was raking his gaze across the mansion for outside movement.

"Well, if you're wantin' French lessons, they can even be a liability, Custis."

The men laughed.

"Shhh—there she is. Pull in tight to the buggy shed."

"My, so secretive," jeered the driver, who pulled the Percheron into the shade of the buggy shed near the rear of the Larimers' immaculately groomed grounds. "This ain't the governor's wife, is it?"

Longarm leaped down off the hansom and jogged out to meet the dark-clad figure running toward him. Cynthia wore a hooded cape, which she held closed across her breasts. She did not say anything as Longarm

helped her up into the cab's single, leather seat. Olafsson had been in the business enough late nights to know when to look away when he should, and he did so now, puffing his fat stogie and taking another pull from his flask.

Longarm pounded the back wall, and Olafsson turned the cab around and pulled it back onto the trail that skirted the perimeter of the Larimer grounds. The heiress snuggled up tight against Longarm, massaging his thigh with her hand and occasionally lifting her chin to press her silky lips against his neck and his cheek.

She smiled up at him when she realized the effect her warm caress on his thigh was having. She could probably feel his pants growing tight across his crotch.

Longarm held her closely but not too closely, as he saw no reason to torture himself unduly until they arrived at his rented flat on the poor side of Cherry Creek. Longarm wasn't sure why the girl wanted to go there. He supposed she found something erotic about venturing into Denver's more raggedy side secretly, under cover of darkness.

When they reached the large rooming house in the upper story of which his small living quarters lay, Cynthia said, "Does the driver have any idea who I am?"

"I don't think so," Longarm said, keeping his voice down. He could smell Olafsson's cigar smoke wafting down from his high perch above and behind him and Cynthia. He could also sense the man's lusty, self-satisfied, half-drunk grin. "Even if he did, I know the feller. He can keep a secret."

"Pay him to wait for me, will you?"

She pulled a black-gloved hand out of the folds of her

black wool cape and pressed a coin into his hand. Longarm looked at the gold eagle that shimmered in the starlight.

"Twenty dollars," he said. "Thanks for not making me feel cheap."

"Tell him he'll earn another one if he waits for me till dawn."

Longarm saw that Olafsson had a blanket tucked under the seat. The man was used to spending the night in his cab—especially after parties on Sherman Avenue, no doubt.

Longarm climbed out of the cab and helped Cynthia down. While she hurried into the concealing shadows of the oaks lining the street, Longarm flipped the coin up to Olafsson, who tested it with his teeth and then gave an impressed grunt.

"Don't do anything I wouldn't do," he told Longarm, grinning around the cigar.

Longarm led Cynthia quietly up the outside steps of the house, careful not to make any loud noises. Longarm's landlady was persnickety, snoopy, and a light sleeper. "Tomcatting on the premises" was against the rules—a rule she'd made up soon after the federal lawman had moved in several years ago.

He and Cynthia had no sooner gotten inside and closed the door than she removed the cape. There she stood before him, her pale skin glistening in the light angling through the curtained windows. Her earrings sparkled. Her breasts looked like two giant mounds of vanilla ice cream pushing up out of the dress's silk corset, just waiting to be devoured.

Chapter 2

Longarm got a lamp burning on his dresser, one corner of which he'd propped on a small plank after its leg had broken off. His bed wasn't made, and there were several old newspapers and empty bottles and dirty dishes strewn about the room's single table and elsewhere.

Cynthia didn't seem to mind. In fact, as he unbuttoned her dress and peeled the straps down her arms from behind, she said, "I love how it smells in here."

He chuckled. He thought she was joking.

"No, I do. It smells like cigars and leather and sweat. Like a man."

"One who can't afford a maid."

As Longarm peeled the dress down to her waist and ran his hands around to her front and cupped her breasts that were still ensconced in a whalebone corset, she waggled her fanny against his groin.

"Mhmmm," she said. "You like me."

Longarm slid her hair back with his nose and sniffed her neck. "Uh-huhh."

She groaned as he poked his tongue in her ear.

"We'd best get you out of this iron maiden," he said, pulling at the corset. "How in Christ . . . ?"

"You've taken it off me before, Custis. You can do it again."

There was a series of buttons and hooks and straps in back that had always given him pause. Fortunately, his raging lust clarified things, and he was peeling the corset open like a cracked walnut and tossing it across the room inside of five minutes.

Cynthia swooned back against him.

Longarm reached around her and slid his hands up her smooth, flat belly to her breasts, which were bare now and all his. He cupped the firm orbs in his hands. Her nipples had already pebbled but now he could feel them standing up against his palms as he massaged her and nuzzled her neck.

At the same time, she continued to grind her bottom against his hips until his raging hard-on, confined by his balbriggans and whipcord trousers, ached.

"Let's get me out of my stockings and panties, and then your turn," Cynthia said, wrestling away from him to sit on the bed and extending a long, pale leg.

Longarm knelt before her and removed the garter belt and panties. Then off came both silk stockings. He leaned forward and shoved his face against the tuft of silky black hair between the tops of her thighs, and worked the tip of his nose between the folds of pink flesh.

Cynthia leaned back on her arms. She threw her head

back and groaned at the ceiling as he ran the tip of his nose against the petal-soft flesh and her clit, which he could feel growing warmer and warmer and more rigid.

Finally, Longarm stood and began unbuttoning his shirt. As he did, the girl rose to a sitting position on the edge of the bed, and, smiling up at him devilishly, her earrings and blue eyes and white teeth sparkling in the light of the lamp, she began unbuttoning his fly.

When he'd gotten his coat, vest, four-in-hand tie, and shirt off and stood before her bare-chested, she opened his pants and was reaching inside the fly of his summer-weight longhandles. She continued to smile up at him playfully, and when she wrapped her slim hand around his cock, she closed her upper teeth down on her bottom lip.

"Got it," she said.

She gently slid it out of his balbriggan fly until it was standing nearly straight up before him, angling the swollen mushroom head back against his belly button.

"Nice," Cynthia cooed. "Oh, gosh . . . so very nice."

She leaned forward and stuck out her tongue. She touched its tip to the swollen head and swirled it gently, slowly.

Longarm drew a breath and leaned his weight back on the low heels of his cavalry stovepipes. Her tongue made his entire cock and his balls tingle. She continued to swirl her tongue against the end of his cock, looking up at him with her erotic gaze before she pulled her head back for a second and then rose a little higher and closed her mouth over the head.

Cynthia's mouth was warm and wet.

Longarm could feel her tongue caressing the

underside of his shaft as she slowly slid her mouth down toward his groin. When she was halfway to his belly, she slid her mouth back off of him and smacked her lips.

Rising from the bed, she shoved him down onto it, and, kneeling naked before him, her pale breasts with their distended nipples jostling—she was wearing only the diamond earrings now—she pulled off each of his boots in turn.

She helped him out of his pants and balbriggans. And when all of his clothes were on the floor around her, she placed her hands on his thighs, leaned forward, grabbed his cock around its base with her right hand, and pumped him gently. After a time, she dropped her mouth down over him and started sucking tenderly at first while holding his cock steady with one hand and cupping his balls with the other.

After about five excruciating minutes of working him over grandly with her lips and tongue, and swallowing him a few times, gagging on the bulbous head, she bobbed her head up and down quickly. She worked him into a raging lather of silently screaming passion.

Longarm leaned back, stretched his arms and legs out, and released a hot geyser of seed into Cynthia's mouth and down her throat. She groaned and moaned and gagged, holding her mouth down stubbornly. He could feel her throat spasming against him as he continued to violently spend himself.

Some of his seed pearled on the tip of her nose.

When he'd finally stopped bucking and grunting against her, causing the bed to squawk, she lifted her mouth and gasped, rubbing the back of a pale hand

across her mouth and nose. Her face was flushed, eyes glazed with tears.

"God, Custis!" she said, "I thought I was gonna drown!"

Longarm could only gasp as he lay there, catching his breath and staring at the ceiling, feeling as though an ore dray had dropped a load of rocks on his chest.

Cynthia rose and walked over to the dresser to pour a glass of water. When she returned, she was carrying a bottle of Tom Moore rye and two water glasses. Longarm sat up as she knelt between his legs again, and she poured them each a drink.

This was how it usually went. She'd suck him, releasing the fervor and torment of his initial lust, and then they'd have a drink together and flirt and snuggle and fondle each other while he recovered. Then they'd get down to the real business, which they got down to about fifteen minutes after his French lesson and after they'd finished their drinks.

She pulled the covers back, drew one of the pillows down beneath her hips, and pointed her beautiful ass in the air. As he scuttled up on his knees between her legs, she reached behind her, wrapped her hand around his cock, and squeezed it several times. When it was rock hard, she lowered her hands to the bed and arched her back, wagging her ass.

"Give it to me, Custis. Every inch of that beautiful ax handle! Every beautiful . . . *ahhh, gawd*!"

"You asked for it."

"Oh, God. Oh, God."

"Shhh. My landlady, darlin'."

"I'll try," Cynthia said throatily, grinding her forehead into the mattress as he hammered against her butt, chomping a cold cigar. "But . . . oh, fuck, Custis . . . oh, *ohhhh-ahhhh . . . !*"

She buried her face in the sheets as he continued grinding away, ramming his cock in and out of her as he held her hips firmly in his large, brown hands.

When she came the first time, she did her best to muffle her love screams, though Longarm was certain that if the old bat downstairs were awake, she'd heard something. She probably wouldn't know what.

The second time he fucked the beautiful heiress, from the missionary position, he had to clamp a pillow over her head when she crested her passion, or she likely would not have only awakened his landlady but everyone else in the house as well as the entire neighborhood down to the stockyards.

Someone might have screamed for the Denver Police.

The lovers had a drink together, sitting up against the wall at the head of the bed, their limbs glued together by sweat. Longarm smoked his cigar. Cynthia took a couple of puffs and coughed, exhaling. They talked drowsily, and when he'd finished his drink and his cigar and was about to nod off, she crawled on top of him, kissed his cock alive once more.

He groaned his objection, but then she fucked him slowly, delicious with her large, firm breasts, raking her jutting nipples against his balls. What little seed he had left jetted across her tits and dribbled down her cleavage. She rolled onto her back and massaged it into her belly.

Later, Cynthia gave them each a cool, leisurely

sponge bath, and then she dressed quietly, kissed him good-bye, turned out the lamp, and left.

Lying belly up and naked on the bed, Longarm was only dimly aware of the clomps of Olafsson's Percheron receding into the distance before he drifted into a deep, pleasantly exhausted sleep.

He had no idea how much time had passed before something grabbed his toe. Still asleep, he tried to pull his foot away, but whoever had ahold of his toe would not release it. He must have been dreaming.

He opened his eyes and lifted his head.

He gasped when he saw the two Indians standing at the foot of his bed.

Chapter 3

Still ensconced in the warm, clinging wool of his slumber, a warning voice in Longarm's ear shouted, *"Attack!"*

Semi-consciously, he was somewhere down in the Arizona or New Mexico desert and his current mission had run him up against a band of savage Apaches. He flung his right hand toward where he'd coiled his shell belt and holstered Colt Frontier .44, well within easy reach, but neither the gun nor the holster was there.

His hand slapped down on rumpled, slightly damp cotton sheets.

And then the wool of sleep lifted enough that he remembered where he was.

Heart still thudding, he turned to stare down over the long length of his muscular, naked body toward the two Indians still standing there—a man and a young woman. The man was slender, with a rough-hewn, craggy, brick-red face and hawk nose framed by long, black hair

liberally stitched with gray. He wore a black, bullet-crowned hat and suspenders over a red calico shirt.

The girl couldn't have been much over twenty, and ravishing—an Apache version of Cynthia Larimer. She wore a shirt much like the man's under a doeskin dress. She wore her long, raven-black hair in braids bound with hawk feathers and rawhide. Her hair glistened with what Longarm, who'd frequented Apache country often, knew to be bear grease.

The man was grinning down at Longarm delightedly, brown eyes reflecting the dawn light pushing through a near window.

"Wait," Longarm grunted, fisting sleep from his eyes and rising to his elbows. *"War Cloud?"*

The Indian chuckled, showing large, off-white teeth between his thick, brown lips. Longarm looked at the Indian girl standing beside his old Indian friend, and he pulled a twisted sheet corner over his exposed crotch.

"What in *hell*?"

War Cloud chuckled. "Get your duds on, Custis—we got a trail to dust!"

"Huh?" Again, Longarm looked at the girl with sexily somber, near-black eyes standing to War Cloud's right.

War Cloud wrapped a proud arm around her shoulders. "Longarm, meet my daughter, Magpie. Magpie, meet my good friend Custis P. Long, the famous deputy United States marshal known as Longarm."

"Pleased to meet you," Longarm said skeptically.

The girl just stared at him.

Longarm said, "How in the hell . . . ?" He looked at the door flanking the Coyotero Apache father and

daughter. They must have come in when Cynthia left, leaving the door unlocked. "How long you been here?"

"Since early last evening. We let ourselves in."

"How?"

War Cloud grinned again proudly, squeezing the girl whose head came up to his shoulder. "Magpie's a sorceress. Some even call her a witch!" He whispered that last.

Longarm's mind was spinning. His sleep-drawn features acquired another incredulous cast as he said, "You mean . . . you been here . . . *all night* . . . ?"

"Yeah, we were sittin' in your kitchen over yonder," War Cloud said, jerking his head back toward the doorway flanking Longarm's dresser. "When you and the lady came in, Magpie thought we should say somethin', but you two seemed to be havin' such a good time an' all"—War Cloud grinned again, widely enough to show a couple of missing back teeth—"that I didn't have the heart to interrupt. We just sat at your kitchen table, Magpie an' me, and ate some jerky and biscuits we had along for the trip. Woulda made coffee, but I didn't find nothin' food-wise but some moldy bread in there."

As Longarm managed to wrap his mind around that War Cloud and his daughter had been in his flat since well before and then well after Longarm and Cynthia had arrived, his lower jaw slowly sagged toward his naked chest. "You mean . . . you heard . . . ?"

"Oh, and *saw*," War Cloud said. "I couldn't help but sneak a peek a time or two. Boy, you an' that purty white lady were really goin' at it, Custis! You still got it—don't you, you old dog!"

Jaw hanging, Longarm just gaped at War Cloud, sliding his shocked, horrified gaze between the old Apache scout and his daughter.

"I do apologize, Custis. I know it weren't officially right. And between bouts I thought we should say somethin', but you two seemed to be havin' so much fun even when you weren't throwin' the blocks to each other, I figured it was a special night, and it was best if me an' Magpie just held our tongues and waited you out."

The Apache shook his head again and grinned. "Boy, you two were sure goin' at it. I gotta tell you, old pal—I was impressed."

War Cloud winked.

Longarm's cheeks and ears were scalding as he glanced at War Cloud's daughter. "Oh, don't worry about Magpie. I figured it was high time she learned about the ways of men an' women. I didn't quite know how I was gonna tell it to her—never been good with that sort of thing, and of course it's all up to me since her ma died so long ago—so I reckon I got you and that Cynthia lady to thank for clearing it all up for her."

A little color rose in Magpie's tan cheeks, but her exotically beautiful features otherwise remained implacable. War Cloud chuckled.

"Hope you still have some strength left. Sounds like you an' me an' Magpie will be foggin' the trail for Arizona soon."

Longarm's embarrassment was so keen that he couldn't hear much more of what the man was saying above the ringing in his ears. He looked around, wanting to rise, but then he looked at his all-but-naked body sprawled in the bed, and then at the girl, and said,

"Uh . . . War Cloud—I reckon it don't matter much, since Magpie already done heard an' seen pretty much everything, but would you two mind headin' back out into the kitchen while I dress? Then maybe you can fill me in about what in the hell you're doin' here, and what all this is about—the three of us headin' to Arizona together . . ."

Honestly, he wasn't sure that his old friend hadn't gone doughy in his thinker box. The last he'd heard, War Cloud had been traveling around the country with Buffalo Bill Cody's Wild West show. Longarm hadn't seen the man in a good ten years. And now old War Cloud shows up in Longarm's living quarters at the rooming house . . . with his *daughter* . . . in the middle of the *night* while Longarm's burying his piston in the princess of Denver!

Longarm crawled out of bed and splashed water in the bowl atop his washstand. He glanced toward the doorway beyond which War Cloud was apparently now sitting at Longarm's kitchen table with Magpie. Longarm shook his head and only vaguely noted the gradual diminishment of the burn of embarrassment in his cheeks and ears.

When he'd bathed, he dressed in his customary working gear—chambray shirt, fawn-colored vest, skintight whipcord trousers, and brown wool frock coat. He set his snuff-brown, low-crowned, flat-brimmed hat on his head, bit the tip off a three-for-a-nickel cheroot, and said through the kitchen door, "All right—I'm decent enough, I reckon, War Cloud. I bet you and Magpie are hungry. What do you say we go out and rustle us up some huevos rancheros?"

* * *

Longarm led the War Clouds down the outside steps of
his flat, and in the milky dawn light he saw that father
and daughter were both armed to the teeth.

War Cloud himself wore two old Army Model .44s
for the cross draw high on his hips and two cartridge
belts. A bowie knife jutted from one of the mule-eared
cavalry boots that was similar in style to Longarm's
own. Over one shoulder he carried an ancient pair of
saddlebags to which a flea-bitten bedroll was strapped.
In his free hand, he carried the same kind of Spencer
repeater he'd carried when he was scouting bronco
Apaches for the army about ten to fifteen years ago,
when Longarm had known him last.

Hell, it was probably the very same, old, single-shot,
breech-loading long gun he'd used while scouting.

In the better light outside, Longarm saw that Magpie
was even more comely than Longarm had at first
thought. Her bust was high and full, belly flat and firm,
hips nicely curved, her legs long and muscular beneath
the doeskin skirt she wore to the tops of her deerskin
moccasins, the high tops of which were folded down in
the tradition of her people. There were several beaded
designs on her dress, the hem of which was outlined
with colored porcupine quills. Between the hem of the
dress and the tops of her boots was an alluring two
inches of bare, dark tan skin.

She, too, was armed for war . . . or at least a battle.
She wore a .44 top-break Schofield in a holster high on
her left hip and a light cartridge belt. On her opposite
hip she wore a bone-handled bowie knife in a beaded

sheath. She did not carry a rifle but held over her left shoulder a pair of saddlebags and blanket roll.

Longarm flagged down a coal wagon—he'd caught rides downtown with most of the coal and firewood haulers, at one time or another—and as he and his guests sat down on the open tailgate and the wagon lurched forward, War Cloud leaned toward Longarm and said, "My daughter, Magpie—she's a purty one, eh, Custis?"

War Cloud had been amongst white men so long that he spoke with only a barely detectable accent.

"About as comely a girl as I've seen, I reckon, War Cloud." Custis cupped a match to the cheroot dangling from between his teeth.

"Tread carefully around her."

Longarm glanced skeptically at his old friend, who sat to his left, Magpie on War Cloud's other side. They dangled their legs over the cobblestones as the Percherons in the coal wagon's traces clomped along in the quiet early morning. "Well, I did see she's damn near as well armed as you are."

War Cloud shook his head. "Like Magpie herself, her mother, Seven Stars in the Sky, was a sorceress. You remember how she hated white men?"

Longarm did remember, and he nodded. Seven Stars had died from smallpox about a year after Longarm had first met War Cloud, down in Arizona Territory, when War Cloud had been chief of Apache scouts at Fort McHenry.

"Before Seven Stars died, she cast a spell to protect her daughter from the White Eyes."

Longarm glanced around his old friend to look at the man's daughter sitting the tailgate stiffly, staring straight ahead at the tree-lined street sliding out from beneath the lurching, swaying wagon. "A spell?"

"A spell, that's right." War Cloud glanced furtively at his daughter and then leaned closer to Longarm and pitched his voice softly. "Any white man who tries to fuck her—his cock will swell up, turn black, and fall off."

"Oh, a spell, eh?" Longarm glanced once more at the man's beautiful daughter and gave a wry snort. "Well, thanks for tellin' me, War Cloud. I do appreciate it."

War Cloud winked. "That's what friends are for, Custis."

They got off on the corner of Colfax and Seventh Avenue, right in the heart of the downtown of the sprawling old cow town, just as the sun was splintering above the eastern plains and spreading a gold-bronze shine across the Front Range of the Rocky Mountains rising about fifteen miles to the west. It was still cool and fresh, but it being August, it would heat up fast.

It wasn't as dry here as it was where War Cloud hailed from originally, in the Southwest, but it was dry enough for Longarm, who this time of the year, when his nose and eyes turned dry as desert dust, always yearned for the silky air of his own home of West-by-God Virginia.

Longarm's habit was to breakfast on the free lunch counter at the Black Cat Saloon, which was in spitting distance of the Federal Building, which wouldn't open until eight o'clock. He was eager as hell to find out from Billy Vail, whom he was due to see at eight o'clock

sharp, just what War Cloud's visit, apparently instigated by Billy himself, was all about.

But until then he'd catch up with his old pal War Cloud, ogle his pretty daughter, try to forget about what the girl's eyes and ears had taken in the night before, and enjoy a cold, refreshing beer with a Tom Moore chaser.

Chapter 4

Longarm hesitated a moment before entering the saloon.

He glanced at War Cloud and Magpie and then looked around for signs banning "Injuns" from the premises. Such signs had once been plentiful around Denver, though Longarm couldn't recollect seeing many in recent years. Denver didn't get a lot of Native visitors these days, since most of the American aboriginals had been confined to reservations far from the West's growing cities.

As he led the War Clouds through the batwings, however, all eyes turned toward them not once but two or three times, and held. Longarm saw the morning bartender, Kenny Dunbar, beetle his red brows as he stared over the polished mahogany, hang his lower jaw, and slowly reach under the bar top no doubt for the hide-wrapped bung starter he kept in the event one of his customers got out of hand.

"Keep your hands above the bar, Ken," Longarm

said, grinning as he sauntered up to the counter. "Do as I say, or you'll lose your topknot."

"They with you, Custis?"

"Ken, meet my old pal, War Cloud and his lovely daughter, Magpie. They're here on business . . . we just don't know what kind yet."

The barman studied the two critically. His eyes melted in their sockets when they perused the Apache princess, who'd stopped about halfway between the batwings and the bar, frowning as she appraised the room.

There were about eight other men in the place—five regulars and three sitting back in the shadows that Longarm didn't recognize. The customers' eyes had found the princess, as well, and even old Jefferson Langtry, who'd fought Indians with Custer, relaxed in his chair and drew up his mouth corners, his rheumy old eyes glittering at the girl's comely figure.

"Well, I'll be," Dunbar rasped.

Longarm ordered a beer for himself and War Cloud. The lawman asked Magpie what she was drinking, and she did not reply but held her gaze on the room, as though every man here was a wildcat about to pounce. War Cloud said, "She doesn't speak much English, Custis. And she doesn't speak to white men, at all. Her mother's blood, you understand."

War Cloud ordered the girl a beer, since she needed the beer to qualify for the free bread, meat, and cheese arranged on a large, round tray halfway down the bar, and a glass of water. When Longarm and his guests had all built sandwiches and were seated at a table near the front of the place, Longarm dumped his shot of rye into

his beer, waited for the foam to subside, and took down a third of the morning elixir in three long swallows.

The girl watched him critically. Longarm didn't think the look was much about the drink. She'd been studying him critically, skeptically, as though she didn't know what to think of him, all morning. But then, she seemed to study the other men in the saloon the same way.

Critically, skeptically, as though she were vaguely suspicious of the intentions of each.

Longarm set the glass back down on the table and tried to ignore her stare. He ran the back of his hand across his lips and longhorn mustache. "All right, now that my thinker box is oiled, maybe I can think straighter about the situation at hand. Any idea why you and Magpie are here, War Cloud?"

"I have no idea, Custis," War Cloud said, hunched over the table and devouring his sandwich like a coyote on a freshly killed rabbit. "I was hoping you would know."

Longarm shook his head as he bit into his own sandwich and glanced at Magpie, who was none-too-daintily eating her own meal while keeping her eyes locked on Longarm—when she wasn't nervously scrutinizing the other men in the room, that was.

Longarm swallowed and said, "I got back from an assignment three days ago. Billy Vail gave me a couple days to cool my heels . . . and, uh . . ."

"Entertain that girl who moans so purty?" War Cloud grinned as he chewed.

"Yeah, somethin' like that," Longarm said, glancing at Magpie and feeling his cheeks burn again.

The truth was, he'd been cavorting with Cynthia

against his boss's advice. Marshal Billy Vail thought that it was only a matter of time before the General and sweet Aunt May found out that his senior-most badge toter was "fucking that moneyed little debutante seven ways from sundown," and Billy would be searching for a replacement for Longarm's job—after the deputy's funeral, of course.

"I haven't seen Billy in several days, but he sent a note to my flat over the weekend, ordering me not to be a minute late to his office this morning, so whatever it is, I reckon we'll find out about it is in about a"— Longarm glanced at the Regulator clock over the bar—"half hour or thereabouts. He must have sent for you while I was out corralling rustlers up around the Wyoming line. When I got back, he was out with a head cold."

Longarm swallowed a bite of his sandwich and washed the bite down with a slug of his drink. "In the meantime, how's Buffalo Bill been treating you, you old coyote?"

War Cloud thought about that gravely while he chewed, hunkered over the thick sandwich he held in both his large, leathery dark hands. "To be honest with you, brother, I was glad to get Billy's telegram. Starting to feel like one of Wild Bill's monkeys. I'm a full-blood Coyotero, but Wild Bill kept making me play a Sioux with a full headdress. General Custer always guns me down at the end of our 'battle.'

"You don't know how tired I was getting of clutching my chest and falling over my horse and having to lay there with his boot on my belly while he makes a big, windy speech about how times are changing. That the

Red Man's time is over and now it's time for the White Man to bring civilization to the New Frontier.

"And what's with that big eagle-feather headdress he makes me wear? Do white people really think we wear those gaudy things when we ride into battle?"

Longarm chuckled. "I reckon they might get in the way a tad." He glanced at Magpie. "She play in the show, too?"

"Magpie was a trick rider. She was good. But she didn't get along with Wild Bill or the other players, and she didn't like having to play Pocahontas. Magpie has no idea who in hell Pocahontas was. Since she won't speak English or talk in any tongue to a white man, the others made fun of her. Wild Bill tried to get frisky with her a time or two." War Cloud kicked Longarm under the table and grinned with half of his broad, dark face. "At his own risk. You understand, amigo?"

Longarm glanced at the girl to his right, who was slowly eating her sandwich and staring at the table. He wondered if she always looked like a wildcat about to snarl and pounce, or if she was nervous about being in a city.

"I take it Wild Bill managed to keep all his body parts?"

"It was close a time or two, brother. I warned the old man. I think the last time he finally got the message." War Cloud shook his head and took a long drink from his beer. "I had to get her out of there. When we're finished up with whatever Billy wants us to do, I'm going to take her back to the mountains in Arizona, stake a claim, maybe build up a ranch somewhere amongst our Coyotero brothers and sisters."

War Cloud looked at his daughter and spoke as though she weren't present though Longarm sensed she understood what her father was saying. "Magpie—she's never had a man. She's a woman now—nineteen years old. Back home, she would have been married years ago. She needs a man. A good Apache warrior. That will take some of the—what is the white man saying? Starch out of her drawers?"

War Cloud chuckled.

Longarm glanced at the black-eyed beauty again. Her eyes met his gaze briefly and then she jerked her eyes back down to the table and buried her teeth in her sandwich. Longarm thought a slight blush touched her fine, smooth, cherry-tan cheeks.

Longarm cleared his throat, ignoring the pull of lust in his groin. "Yeah, that oughta take care of it."

"Hey, brother, you catch this?" War Cloud said in voice so low that Longarm had barely heard it.

"Uh . . . yup."

He'd been aware of the three men at the back of the room since he and the War Clouds had entered the saloon. Now those three men had gained their feet and were donning their hats.

One was strolling along the bar toward Longarm and the War Clouds a little too slowly, with a little too much ease. Feigned ease.

He was whistling softly and checking the time on a pocket watch. Another of the three was just now leaving their table and walking slowly toward the far side of the room, also whistling and pretending to be staring at a large oil painting of a naked woman sprawled on a red feinting couch hanging on the wall opposite the bar.

"Who you think they're after," Wolf Cloud said, chewing the last of his sandwich, his dark eyes dancing delightedly. "You . . . me . . . or Magpie?"

"I don't know—should we draw straws?"

"I'm guessin' you since this is your town."

"If you keep your eyes on the one behind me, I'll keep my eyes on the one behind you."

"Okay." War Cloud polished off his beer while keeping a dark eye on the man appraising the canvas hanging from the wall behind Longarm and to the lawman's right. "Magpie is watching the third man."

Longarm had glimpsed the third one, who now had his foot up on the chair he'd been sitting in, frowning down at the toe of his right boot, which he was rubbing with a red neckerchief, as though to remove a stain. He wasn't making a very good show of it. He kept rolling his cunning gaze toward Longarm's table.

Longarm looked at Magpie. She'd finished her sandwich nearly as quickly as her father did. Now she sniffed and swiped the back of her left hand across her mouth and nose and tossed one of her braids back behind her shoulder.

She kept her right hand beneath the table. She had not touched her beer, but now she picked up her water glass between her thumb and index finger, curiously extending her pinky, and took two swallows. She rolled a fleeting glance at Longarm.

Longarm was afraid for the girl. The last thing he wanted to do was get War Cloud's daughter killed because three curly wolves had recognized him as a lawdog who'd done them wrong sometime in the past. It wasn't an unusual situation. Longarm had been in the

man-hunting business long enough to have piss-burned quite a few men.

The third man, to Longarm's left, set his right boot down on the floor with a grunt and said casually, "All right, fellas—I'm ready now!"

"Sounds good to me, Buford," said the man behind War Cloud, turning from the bar that he'd been facing as though perusing the bottles lined up on the back bar shelves.

Just then, Longarm recognized his bearded face with its too-close eyes and scarred lower lip. Chet Fordham grinned at the man behind Longarm and said in a voice that echoed around the cavernous drinking hall, "You ready, Willie?"

"Everybody down!" Longarm shouted as Fordham swept up two long-barreled Smith & Wessons and squinted down both barrels at Longarm.

As the bushwhacker shouted, "Die, you son of a bitch, die!" Longarm threw himself left out of his chair, noting in the periphery of his vision that the other customers in the room, having sensed trouble, flung themselves to the floor.

Fordham's Smith & Wessons roared, lapping flames toward Longarm's now-empty chair. At the same time, the man behind Longarm fired his own pistols at the chair that had just been vacated by War Cloud.

Longarm hit the floor behind a table and rolled up off his left shoulder, rising to a crouch and extending his double-action Colt Frontier .44 at Fordham. Grimacing, he cut loose with three quick shots.

He watched through his own geysering orange flames and puffing powder smoke the outlaw he'd once put

away in the Wyoming Territorial Prison for selling poison whiskey to the Arapahos, screaming and stumbling back against the bar, shooting his matched Smithies into the pressed-tin ceiling over Longarm's table.

Longarm shot him again. The cutthroat screamed again, dropped his shooting irons, turned to grab the edge of the bar, couldn't hold himself, and collapsed to the floor with a thud.

Longarm wheeled in time to see the second shooter dancing back against the naked lady he'd been ogling, triggering both of his own pistols into the floor. He dropped to his knees, loosed a bellow at the ceiling, blood pumping from the two holes over his heart, and fell face forward without even cushioning his fall with his hands.

Two cutthroats were down.

Longarm wheeled to face the third man, aiming his cocked revolver straight out from his shoulder. The man stood near the table at which all three had been sitting. Longarm didn't think the man had gotten off a shot. At least, Longarm hadn't heard a report from the third man's direction.

Longarm eased the tension in his trigger finger. The man was slowly loosening his hold on the Colt .45 in his right hand. He was blinking rapidly and crossing his eyes slightly as he stared up, aghast, at the horn handle of the thick bowie knife protruding from the dead middle of his forehead. Blood oozed from the deep cut made by the knife blade driven into his skull and shone darkly in the morning light pushing through the saloon's front windows.

He fell straight back as though all his bones had

turned to jelly, then slammed onto the table behind him with a loud, crunching thud.

Lowering his Colt, Longarm turned to rake his gaze across War Cloud to Magpie, who still crouched about five feet back in the same crouch as when she'd whipped the savage blade out of its scabbard and sent it careening into the third man's head. Her jaws were hard, lips pursed, eyes sharp. Her cheeks were beautifully flushed.

Slowly, she straightened. Longarm stared at her, his lower jaw hanging.

She glanced at him, glanced at her father. War Cloud gave her an approving nod. Magpie strode forward, weaving around the tables. She leaped catlike onto the table on which the third man lie, his arms and legs hanging over the sides, glassy eyes staring at the ceiling.

She stared down at the dead man and then reached down to wrap both hands around the bowie knife's stout horn handle. She set her left moccasin against the man's chest and used it for leverage as, with a loud grunt, she pulled the blade out of the man's skull. It made a wet grinding, sucking sound.

Magpie leaped to the floor, cleaned the bloody blade off on the front of the dead man's wool vest, and returned it to her belt sheath.

The five other customers, still on the floor between Longarm and the third dead man and Magpie, peered over their respective tables with wary amazement at the Apache girl with the dead-eye bowie-knife aim.

Magpie strode between Longarm and her father, heading for the batwings and saying something in her guttural tongue over her shoulder. She went out, the batwings clacking behind her.

Longarm turned to War Cloud. "What'd she say?"

"Magpie said she is tired of white men and their smelly cities and that she was happy to send that white man to the spirit world with one hell of a headache." The Apache laughed. "I told you she was somethin'."

Longarm looked at Dunbar scowling red-faced over the top of his bar. The apron appraised the blood-spattered room and then turned his angry glare on the federal lawman. "Custis, you're damn close to getting yourself barred from the premises!"

Chapter 5

Longarm smoothed Dunbar's feathers by assuring him that he'd see to it that the saloon owner would be promptly and thoroughly reimbursed for damages. He told one of the two street cops who came running at the sound of the shots that he'd explain later.

Of course, the Denver Police force all knew Longarm. A man who'd been bushwhacked as many times as Longarm had in their fair city carried quite a reputation that likely wouldn't have set so well on the overworked, underpaid local badge toters if they didn't also know that he was Chief Marshal Billy Vail's senior-most deputy who had sent a long list of bad men to either cold, dark graves or the nearly as cold and dark federal prison.

Of course, the whole dustup had been instigated by the bushwhackers, and Dunbar would tell the bluecoats that, anyway, so Longarm's signature on a brief affidavit would tidy everything up in no time. The matter would

be settled before the men were sent home for burial or planted in Denver's pauper cemetery.

Despite the interruption, Longarm and the War Clouds were only fifteen minutes late as they headed for their meeting with Billy Vail, who was so accustomed to Longarm being late anyway that he likely would have had a heart stroke if the rangy deputy had been prompt on so fair and sunny a midsummer morning.

On the short stroll to the Federal Building from the Black Cat, they were met with quite a few dubious stares. Most folks in Denver probably had never seen an Apache before, and they likely hadn't spied so obvious a pair of Indians—one a beautiful Indian princess— walking the cinder-paved sidewalks in a month of Sundays.

Young boys hocking newspapers on street corners; drivers of hansom cabs, ranch wagons, and beer wagons; suited businessmen heading for their shops; office girls scurrying to work in their summer-weight frocks; even stray dogs hunting mice or food scraps around boardwalks—all strained their necks to watch the unlikely threesome pass and then head on up the Federal Building's broad, stone steps.

The trio headed through the cavern-like halls, Longarm sucking a cold cheroot, War Cloud father and daughter for the most part staring straight ahead. War Cloud himself paused to shake hands with a couple of other deputy marshals who'd worked with the Coyotero when he'd been a tracker on the government payroll.

Longarm pushed through the heavy wooden, glass-paned door marked simply U.S. MARSHAL and stepped

to one side to hold the door wide for his guests. Billy Vail's prissy secretary, Henry, glanced over his narrow shoulder as his long, pale hands continued to tap away on his infernally loud typewriting machine that he loved so much, and said with his customarily droll air, "You're late again, Deputy Lo—"

The clattering stopped abruptly as Henry's bespectacled eyes found the Apaches. Chief Marshal Billy Vail's personal secretary leaped out of his chair as though his pants had suddenly caught fire and twirled around, eyes snapping wide. His gaze flicked between his two Apache guests before returning to War Cloud, and then a crimson flush rose in his cheeks, and he said with no small relief, "Mr. War Cloud!"

"What'd you think, Henry?" Longarm asked. "We were under attack?"

"Well, it's just been . . . so . . . long since . . ."

War Cloud laughed and stepped forward, shoving a big, brown paw across the young man's immaculate desk and saying, "Ain't no mister in it now any more than there ever was, Henry, but just the same, it's nice to see you again."

"Nice to see you, too, War Cloud," Henry said, shaking the Indian's hand. His eyes returned to the girl standing back against the door and near the hat tree onto which Longarm had tossed his hat. "And . . . this is . . . ?"

Longarm grinned as Henry's normally coolly dismissive gaze raked the girl up and down and sideways. Longarm had always suspected the lad might have been a Nancy-boy, but now, seeing Henry's face mottle red and his eyes nearly pop out of his head at the vision of

the Apache princess before him, Longarm thought he'd have to revise his estimation.

War Cloud introduced his daughter to Henry, but while the lad leaned over his desk to extend his hand toward Magpie, the girl merely stood back by the door, regarding him with her cool disdain, arms crossed on her breasts.

"Oh," Henry said, awkwardly lowering his hand.

"She ain't much of a hand shaker," War Cloud explained. "Most Apaches ain't. I been around white men long enough to understand the gesture, but most Apaches would fall down laughing if you extended your hand to 'em. Magpie—she just ignores such ceremony, but she don't mean nothin' personal by it."

The frosted-glass door flanking the other side of the secretary's desk suddenly opened, and Billy Vail stepped out to say, "I thought I heard familiar voices out here. War Cloud—welcome back!"

The frumpy, balding chief marshal, customarily attired in a wrinkled white shirt and brown wool vest with dangling watch chain, strode out to give the Apache's hand a brisk shake. "Glad you could make it," Vail said. "I wasn't sure you received my message—I know how you never were one to reply to a telegram, so I was just keeping my fingers crossed."

Since War Cloud didn't know how to read or write, he pretty much just ignored all situations in which either activity was required. If you sent him a telegram, you'd never know he got it until you saw him again.

He said, "Nice to see you again, Chief. Yeah, I got it, and I was glad. I was waitin' on an excuse for me an' Magpie to head west again. I'm afraid Chicago an' them

other cities back East—they just aren't for this old redskin."

"Daughter?" Billy was staring at Magpie, the skin above the bridge of his nose wrinkling. "Say, I heard about you havin' a daughter, War Cloud. That's right—she's why you left the service. Say . . . that's some girl you got there, mister . . ."

"Don't try to shake her hand, Chief," Longarm advised, standing back by the hat tree near the Apache princess. "She might crack a bone or two."

Billy nodded as he continued to study the girl, obviously impressed by her, as any male—even a chubby, balding, long-married, middle-aged one—would be. The chief marshal sighed and glanced between Longarm and War Cloud, "Well, I'm glad you two ran into each other—or did you just get here at the same time?"

"Oh, no, Chief," Longarm said. "We sorta ran into each other last night. *Late* last night. In my flat over on the raggedy side of Cherry Creek. Good thing ole War Cloud still remembered where it was." The deputy's tone was ironic.

War Cloud grinned. Longarm thought he heard Magpie give a snort. A barely audible snort but a snort just the same though she didn't look at him.

"Okay—well, anyway," the chief marshal said, obviously a little confused but seeing no point in having the matter clarified, which was just fine with Longarm. The chief marshal clearly had more important things on his plate. "Why don't you two come on into my office, and I'll give you the one-two-three. Nasty business down in your home country, War Cloud. That's why I was hoping you'd come."

"Had a feelin' that was why, Chief."

As Billy turned to walk into his office, he glanced over his shoulder. Magpie was walking toward him, a few steps behind Longarm. "She might as well stay out here with Henry," Vail said. "She wouldn't have no interest in hearin' about this mess."

"She might as well hear about it, Chief," War Cloud said, holding the door open. "She'll be comin' with me an' Custis. Me an' Magpie are heading home and, besides, I taught Magpie to be every bit the tracker her old man is. She is, too. And her eyes are sharp as an eagle's."

"She's right good with a bowie knife, too, Chief," Longarm wryly interjected, not bothering to explain the matter of the three dead men over at the Black Cat Saloon.

Billy looked at the girl once more, speculatively, nodding. "You don't say. Well, all right. I have only one chair, but you fellas can sit on the floor."

Vail chuckled at that as he walked on into his office. But when they were all inside, Magpie ignored Longarm's gesture for her to sit in the chair and sat on the floor, her back against the door, arms crossed on her breasts. War Cloud shrugged, then grinned as he himself took the chair.

Longarm stood against the room's outside wall, arms crossed on his chest, one boot cocked over the other, the cold cigar still angling from his mouth. He wasn't sure why, but he suddenly had a bad feeling about what his next assignment was going to be. It was probably because he'd learned he'd be heading into the searing Arizona heat at high summer.

That was like heading to hell with the fires still burning.

Also, his old friend War Cloud had been called in special. That likely meant Apache trouble. And Apache trouble was usually the worst kind of trouble of all.

Yes, he had a bad, bad feeling . . .

That was like heading to hell with the fire still
burning.

Also, his old friend West Loud had been called in
special. That ubally meant Apache trouble. And Apache
trouble was usually the worst kind of trouble of all.

Yes, he had a bad, bad feeling.

Chapter 6

Chief Marshal Billy Vail regarded Magpie skeptically where she squatted against his door, and then he plopped his two hundred pudgy pounds down into his high-backed leather chair.

He reached for a handkerchief and blew his nose. "Nothing worse than a cold in the summer." He looked at War Cloud sitting straight across from him in the chair, and then at Longarm standing against the wall. "Looks like old times—don't it, fellas?"

War Cloud slapped his arms down on the arms of the chair. "Feels good to be back, Chief."

"Any chance you'll stay on? We can still use good trackers, War Cloud."

"Nah. I want to take my girl back to Arizona, try my hand at ranching the white man's way. None of that reservation living for me. I want to raise wild horses and sell them to the cavalry for remounts. That would be a good life for both of us."

War Cloud was one of the few Apaches who'd been given written amnesty from President Johnson, excepting him and his daughter from being confined to a reservation. The request had been made by General Crook, who'd found War Cloud's help "extraordinary and invaluable" while leading thirty other Apache scouts during the Tonto Basin campaign against the Tonto Apaches in the '70s. It was also Crook who had recommended War Cloud to be employed by the U.S. marshals as a professional scout and tracker.

"Sounds like a good idea." Vail glanced at the window beside Longarm through which the rumble of morning foot and horse traffic was emanating, as well as the clanging of train bells and the panting of locomotives from down at Union Station. "This city keeps getting louder and stinkier every day. I'm of a mind to join you."

The chief marshal waved his hand in front of his face, dismissing the subject. "Anyway, we'd best move on to the business at hand. Your train will be pullin' out in a couple hours."

Vail plucked a manila envelope off one of many large stacks hiding his cluttered desk and tossed it onto the corner nearest Longarm. "The report's in there but you can't take it with you, Custis. You're gonna have to read it here and digest the information in it before you go."

"Sounds serious, Chief," Longarm said, scratching a match to life on a corner of the desk near the file. "You wanna give us the rundown?"

"It's ugly business. If I was either one of you fellas, I wouldn't wanna have no part in it. Custis, you got no choice, but War Cloud, of course you do. But I hope

you'll take the assignment just the same. I need you on this one. Need you bad, as it concerns a part of the country you know like the back of your hand."

Longarm blew a plume of smoke at the far wall and said, "Billy, you're makin' me right curious. Could you spit it all out for us so me an' War Cloud can stop guessin'."

Vail leaned forward and blew his nose. He cursed under his breath, swiped the handkerchief across his red, raw nose once more, and then leaned back in his chair. "The trouble concerns Fort McHenry down in Arizona. I know you both know where it is—especially you, War Cloud, since you were chief of the Coyotero scouts back there during the '70s."

War Cloud nodded, frowning gravely.

"And you likely know the Mescalero scout, Black Twisted Pine."

"Of course. We were partners, Black Twisted Pine and me despite that our tribes—the Coyoteros and the Mescaleros—were once blood enemies."

"Black Twisted was working with the scouts at Fort McHenry, which isn't much these days since the Apache problem has been dwindling except for old Geronimo himself and a few other bands that don't cotton to the reservation life—which I can fully understand. Rotten damn system, if you ask me, and I know you wouldn't argue the point, War Cloud."

War Cloud said nothing. His dark eyes said exactly what he thought about the federal government confining his people to reservations and trying to turn the hunter-gatherer natives into farmers, and even sending a good many to reservations as far away as Florida and

Oklahoma. It was true that he'd hunted down many of
his own, but only those Apaches he considered blood
enemies, and only because he'd known that the end was
coming for all Apaches, and he'd wanted to end the
fighting.

Also, being Apache, he'd been born a warrior. And
warring had really been all he'd ever known.

"Fort McHenry is still there along Wild Horse Creek,
between the Chiricahua Mountains and the Dragoons,
protecting the ranchers and miners in that neck of the
desert. The commanding officer there is one Major
Anson Belcher. His wife is Lucille Belcher. Lucille
McPherson Belcher."

Vail stopped and regarded each man in turn, as
though waiting for their reaction to the name. Longarm
glanced at War Cloud and shrugged. War Cloud hiked
a shoulder, as well.

"The name supposed to mean somethin' to us,
Chief?" Longarm asked.

"I thought it would ring a bell, since McPherson is
the name of the territorial governor of Arizona. Everett
McPherson."

"All right," Longarm said, growing more and more
impatient with his boss's slow, meandering way of telling him what his assignment was going to be. Billy was
usually much more direct than this. That he wasn't being
as straightforward now caused his senior deputy vague
apprehension.

It meant that the trouble down Arizona way was
either especially complicated or especially dangerous.
Most likely, both.

"I don't understand what this has to do with my old

partner, Black Twisted Pine." War Cloud, normally one of the most patient people Longarm had ever known, was apparently growing as impatient with the chief marshal's slow spiel as Longarm was.

"I don't know if you've seen Black Twisted Pine recently, War Cloud," Vail said, "but I assume you haven't. He was wounded a little over a year ago in a skirmish with some of Geronimo's band. A war lance shattered his knee. He can still use it, I'm told, but for his own safety he was temporarily taken out of the scouting service.

"They kept him on active duty by making him a striker, a personal assistant, to Mrs. Lucy Belcher, in the home she of course shared with Major Belcher. To make my long story a little shorter, she and Black Twisted Pine appeared to have struck up a romance— one that culminated in the two running off together to Mexico."

Longarm looked at War Cloud. He'd always known when War Cloud was astonished because the scout's dark eyes grew a little larger, and his lips parted slightly. Both those things were happening now in the Indian's broad face. As for Magpie, she simply sat with her back against the door, arms extended straight across her upraised knees.

She was staring at the floor between her and Vail's desk. She might have been meditating, but Longarm had a feeling she'd been taking in everything that Vail had said. Like most traditional Apaches, she rarely betrayed her inner reaction to anything.

Longarm said, "Where'd they go, Billy?"

"Into the Shadow Montañas—a little range just south

of the border. They're an extension of the Chiricahuas but on the other side of the line."

"A sacred range to the Chiricahuas," War Cloud said. He glanced over his right shoulder to speak in Apache to his daughter, who again did not react to what she heard. Turning his head forward again, War Cloud translated: "The People of the Turtle Heart."

Vail blew his nose. He sighed as though weary of the cold and his sore, red nose, and flopped back in his chair, making a sour face. "This is serious trouble, gentlemen. Governor McPherson is a proud man, and a hater of the Apache. Lucy's husband, Major Belcher, was cut from the same cloth. Both soldiered during the Little Misunderstanding Between the States. Both come from wealthy Yankee families.

"Major Belcher has been cuckolded, made to look the fool in front of all his men, and he's understandably furious. He's wanting to send American soldiers across the border after his wife and Black Twisted Pine, and both he and his father-in-law have requested that he be given War Department permission to do just that. The permission wasn't granted, and so far both Belcher and McPherson have restrained themselves. They know that to send soldiers into sacred Apache territory—a small band of whom are still living up there in them mountains—could very well fan the flames of the Apache Wars, have them raging back to the level they were at in the late sixties.

"Besides, the Mexicans are damn protective of their border these days, since a gang of desperadoes— deserters from the American cavalry—have been on the loose down there, raiding mines and robbing trains an'

such. These days, no American soldier is allowed across the border. However, in the weeks since those two— Black Twisted Pine and Mrs. Belcher—ran off together, the U.S. Marshals Service was brought in.

"And you two gentlemen, and only you, have been granted permission from President Johnson himself to scuttle on across the border and to do everything you can to *quietly*, without the Mexicans learning about it and without ruffling the feathers of those bronco Apaches living up there in the Shadow Montañas, run down Mrs. Belcher, and bring her back to Fort McHenry.

"Kicking and screaming, if you have to. She has to be brought back to her husband and her father at all costs. This is a great embarrassment to two important men. If she's not brought back, I'm afraid those two men are going to take the bull by the horns, and we're gonna have another major Indian war on our hands."

Longarm took a couple of pensive puffs off his cigar. "Can't they transfer Belcher out of there, Boss? Bring in a new commanding officer?"

"They tried that. Didn't try very hard, though, I don't think. Both Belcher and Governor McPherson have friends in high places, don't you know, and none of his senior officers have pushed very hard to have him transferred. I've heard before that McPherson's wife is a not-too-distant relation to the president. So if the eastern press got wind of this, it would be more than just Belcher and McPherson embarrassed by it. I've no doubt that the president himself wants Mrs. Belcher returned to the major as soon as possible."

Vail sniffed. "So, there you have it, Gentlemen. Henry has travel vouchers all typed out and waiting.

You'll be heading south on the one o'clock flier. You'll pick up remounts at Fort Dryer in New Mexico, and ride to Fort McHenry. I'm allowing a little over a week for travel. In this heat, you'll probably wanna travel mostly at night, but I'll leave that up to you. You been through this before."

Vail studied War Cloud. "What's your answer, my friend? Will you take the job? You know that country like the back of your hand, since you scouted it for years. None of the scouts at the fort knows the border country well at all. If anyone can track them two lovebirds down quickly and quietly, without ruffling the Apaches' feather, you can. I'm offering two dollars and fifty cents a day plus traveling expenses."

War Cloud nodded gravely. "I knew before me and Magpie left Chicago I'd be taking the job, Chief. Even before I knew what the job was about. I knew you would not call me back into the service without good reason. But now, knowing what the job entails—Black Twisted Pine is my adopted brother, and I do not wish to see him hurt—I'll go. And I promise I'll do everything I can to bring the woman back to the major . . . as long as I am not expected to kill my Chiricahua brother, Black Twisted Pine."

"The reason I'm sending you, my friend, is so that can be avoided. Being the man's ex-scouting partner, you're the one man who has a chance to convince him that no matter how strongly he feels about Mrs. Belcher, he has to release her—for his and her own good and for the good of his own people."

Vail glanced at Longarm. "The job of you two men is to bring Mrs. Belcher back to her husband—preferably

before the eastern press gets wind of it and embarrasses not only the major and the governor, but the president himself."

Longarm said, "What if this Mrs. Belcher don't wanna go back to her husband, Chief?"

Vail dipped his chin and gave his senior deputy a stern, commanding look. "You flash them big brown eyes of yours and change the lady's mind. If you don't bring her back, someone else likely will—and then there'll be hell to pave and no hot pitch!"

"All right, all right."

"Oh, by the way." Vail sniffed and looked sheepish. "If you fellas get caught by the Mexicans over there, or if you run into trouble with the Apaches, don't expect any help. 'Cause you won't get it. Those are orders from the president himself."

Chapter 7

Four days later, in the hot desert dusk, Magpie glanced over to where Longarm and War Cloud lay back against their saddles, hats tipped over their eyes. Apparently believing both men were asleep, the young Apache princess let her calico blouse slip down off her shoulders.

However, Longarm was not asleep.

He'd awakened when the girl had risen from her bedroll, just after the sun had gone down. In the summer in the desert Southwest, travelers rode by night, especially when there was a moon, as there was now. That way said travelers spared themselves as well as their mounts from the merciless sun.

Longarm had been sleeping with the intention of rising with the moon, but Magpie had risen first.

The girl's stirring had awakened Longarm. Apparently, she had decided to refresh herself at the *tinaja,* the small stone tank tucked away in this narrow, rocky

arroyo in which they'd set up camp earlier that morning.

The tank was fed by a trickle of spring water. Narrowing one eye as he stared out from beneath his downcanted hat, Longarm saw the girl drop to her knees on the small pool's opposite side, facing him. She glanced up once more, looking toward him.

He closed his eye.

He felt properly chagrined, and more than a little childish, but he didn't want to interrupt the girl's ministrations. Also, the boy inside him and in all men couldn't help wanting to sneak a proscribed peek at her wares.

She was awfully set up, after all. High-busted and long-legged, and though her father had claimed she'd never been with a man, she was one of the most erotically charged young women Longarm had ever known. Aside from Cynthia Larimer, of course . . .

His eyes closed beneath his hat brim, Longarm heard the faint tinkle of dripping water. He opened his eye and peered out from beneath his hat at the girl kneeling on the other side of the pool. She'd slid her doeskin dress and her calico blouse down to her waist and was slowly, quietly cupping water to her chest.

Longarm's conscience forced him to close his eyes. The little boy in him, however, castigated his more mature self for his discretion. "Ah, go ahead and peek," the voice said. "What can it hurt?"

The urgings of his grown-up loins were even more convincing.

Shamefully, he opened his right eye again. Magpie had removed her hair from its customary twin braids, and her long, stygian tresses hung forward over her

shoulders as she cupped water in her right hand and raised that hand to her left breast.

Longarm could catch only a glimpse of the precious orb in the dim light and through the thin, jostling screen of her hair, but what he saw prodded his loins with a sharp, invisible knife. As she dipped her other hand in the water and brought it up to rub the cool, refreshing liquid across her other breast, she straightened her back and lifted her chin.

Her hair slid back slightly to hang straight down her sides, nearly to her belly, completely exposing her breasts that stood up proudly against her chest. They were slightly oblong and firm, with large, alluringly dark areolas and red-brown nipples that appeared slightly distended and pointed a little to each side.

Magpie lifted her chin higher, crossing her arms on her chest and cupping her breasts in each hand. She rolled the nipples between her thumbs and index fingers, and gave a barely audible groan.

Longarm heard a grunt rise up from around the hard knot in his throat. The girl dropped her chin quickly to stare across the water at him, flattening her hands out on her breasts, covering them. Longarm squeezed his eyes closed and tensed.

He pricked his ears, listening.

Had she heard him grunt?

He lay there, his senses attuned, keeping both eyes squeezed shut. His cheeks burned with embarrassment. From across the spring pool he heard a faint rustling sound, as though the girl was covering herself. He heard the faint crackling of her moccasins on the sand around the pool.

The crackling grew louder.

Then it stopped.

Longarm sensed the girl standing over him. Feigning sleep, he kept his face muscles relaxed beneath the hat and tried very hard to keep his breaths long and even.

"You damn fool," his more mature self silently scolded the devilish child inside him.

He steeled himself to receive a kick. None came. He felt the skin above the bridge of his nose furrow, and he was about to open his eyes, but then he kept them closed when he felt a cool drop of water land on his closed lips. Another cool drop landed on the tip of his nose.

Water from the girl's hair, no doubt.

The notion caused his trouser snake to stir in its lair, but he kept his eyes closed despite his nearly over-whelming desire to open them and see just what in the hell she was doing up there.

At the same time he remembered War Cloud's admo-nition to stay away from her unless he wanted his dick to turn black and fall off. Longarm hadn't taken the warning literally, but part of him couldn't help wonder-ing about it just enough to make Magpie all the more alluring.

All the more alluring for being forbidding.

When he heard the soft crackling of sand again, he opened his eye. She was walking away from him. She sat down by her gear about ten feet to his right, and crossed her legs Indian-fashion, and began plaiting her hair. Her blouse was buttoned, and she'd drawn her dress up to her shoulders.

She looked at him, and he thought he saw a smug little smile quirk her lips that were normally a knife

slash across her beautiful face. Longarm reached up and shoved his hat back off his forehead. He sat up with a grunt, as though just waking.

"Oh, you up, Magpie?" he said, stretching.

The girl said nothing. She merely continued to braid her hair while watching him blandly though with what he detected as a knowing light in her molasses-dark, almond-shaped eyes.

"Shoulda woke me," Longarm told the girl, seeing the half-moon angling up over the toothy ridges silhouetted against the soft, spruce-green, southeastern sky. He reached over to his left and nudged War Cloud, still snoring beneath his black, felt, bullet-crowned hat.

"Come on, amigo. Rise an' shine—we're burnin' moonlight."

Several hours later, not long before dawn, they were following an old freight road through the broad, greasewood stippled valley between the Chiricahua Mountains on the left and the Dragoons on the right. War Cloud drew back on the reins of the grulla he'd requisitioned at Fort Dryer in New Mexico, and sat his saddle tensely.

Longarm, riding to the scout's left, also drew rein. Magpie stopped her own buckskin behind the two men.

Longarm glanced at War Cloud and said quietly, "What is it, amigo?"

"Do you feel it?"

"Them long fingernails been raking the back of my neck for the last ten minutes—that what you're talkin' about?"

War Cloud stared straight ahead toward a low, boulder-strewn ridgeline sitting perpendicular to the trail, about fifty yards ahead. The trail had been blasted

through the middle of the outcropping, forming a gray notch straight ahead in the moon-washed, purple ridge.

Longarm looked around, as did War Cloud.

The night was eerily quiet. The moon was quartering low in the northwest, casting an eerie, pearl light from behind Longarm's right shoulder and over the scattered boulders, mesquites, saguaros, and greasewood clumps. Stars flickered like distant campfires.

There was not a breath of breeze stirring the refreshingly cool desert air.

A lone coyote had been baying for the past fifteen minutes.

Nearly straight ahead, a pinprick of light flashed.

"Ambush!" Longarm shouted, reaching forward to yank his Winchester '73 from the scabbard strapped over the right stirrup of his McClellan saddle.

As the bullet screeched off a rock about two feet ahead on his left, the rifle's distant crackle reached his ears. He leaped out of his saddle, as his two trail mates did likewise, and slammed his rifle's butt against the coyote dun's left hip, sending the horse galloping off to the right with the others, out of the line of fire.

Another rifle flashed just right of the first bushwhacker's gun. As the bullet plumed dust in front of him, Longarm dropped to a knee in the trail, raised his rifle, and squeezed off four quick rounds at the ridge.

War Cloud, crouched to Longarm's right, did the same, and when his reports stopped echoing, Longarm ran off the left side of the trail, yelling, "I'm goin' in!"

Behind him, he heard War Cloud shout in his Coyotero tongue at Magpie. Longarm knew enough of the language to know he'd told the girl to stay with the

horses, so they wouldn't run far. Then he glimpsed War Cloud dashing through the desert and paralleling Longarm off the trail's right side, heading for the ridge.

The bushwhackers opened up with their rifles but they obviously couldn't see the two men charging toward them, weaving separate courses around the wiry brown brush clumps, cholla cactus patches, and boulders. Their slugs struck wild, spanging wickedly off rocks or snapping branches.

Running hard, Longarm gained the base of the ridge and didn't slow his pace much as he lunged up the side, loosing sand and gravel in his wake. One of the rifles flashed ahead and on his right, three bullets kicking up gravel well behind him. The shooter could now hear him, maybe see his shadow, but he couldn't track him.

Longarm skipped off several boulders, leaped a low barrel cactus, and skipped off another boulder as he reached the razorback ridge between a one-armed saguaro on his left and a horse-sized and -shaped chunk of rock on his right. He pressed his shoulder to the side of the boulder, thumbing back his rifle hammer.

Breath raked in and out of his lungs from the hard climb. He steadied his hands on his rifle. An eerie silence had fallen in the wake of the shooting. Longarm could sense the tension in the bushwhackers. They knew they'd been run up on; they just didn't know where the runners were.

Longarm consciously slowed his breathing, pricking his ears.

Gravel crackled somewhere ahead and right, along the crest of the ridge he was on. One of the shooters was moving toward him.

He crouched low, took one step forward, and looked around behind the boulder. A shadow moved down the slope and right. Starlight glistened off a rifle barrel. Longarm saw a sombrero silhouetted against the sky. The bushwhacker saw him at the same time and jerked his rifle up.

Longarm aimed and fired.

The man screamed. His own rifle crashed, lapping flames at a slant toward the ground. The ricochet plowed into the end of the boulder near Longarm as the man in the sombrero screamed *"Mierda!"* and staggered backward down the slope, spurs chinging.

A rifle barked farther right along the ridge, and Longarm pumped a fresh cartridge into his own Winchester but held fire when an answering flash and belch evoked a grunt and sent more spurs to ringing raucously.

Longarm called, "War Cloud?"

"Here, Custis," came the Indian's deep voice.

A half second later, another rifle flashed out of the darkness on the downslope ahead of Longarm and on his left—about forty yards away. The bullet burned a line across the lawman's left cheek. He wheeled and, crouching, gritting his teeth, emptied his Winchester, the spent cartridges clinging off the boulder behind him.

He lowered the gun and ran down the slope, following a path that the moon- and starlight revealed between brush clumps and rocks. Ahead, he saw the jostling shadow of the man he'd opened up on moving away. The closer Longarm got to the gent, the clearer the man's grunts and groans became as he ran in the opposite direction. His gait grew more and more shambling.

Finally, he stopped and half fell against a rock.

"Hold it!" Longarm shouted, palming his Colt.

He wanted the man alive. He wanted to know who the shooters were and what had prompted the ambush.

"Fuck you, you son of a bitch!" the man screamed.

Light flashed off the barrel of the rifle that the hombre was swinging toward Longarm. The lawman extended his Colt Frontier and hurled two chunks of .44-caliber lead at the dead center of the man. The bullets punched him straight back. He dropped his rifle and flailed at the rock to no avail.

He piled up on the ground beyond it with a shrill cry. There were wild snapping sounds. The man groaned, gasped frantically. When Longarm reached the wounded bushwhacker, he saw what the commotion had been. The man had fallen into a sprawling cholla and been impaled by a thousand of the jumping cactus's porcupine-like quills.

He lay quivering as he died, blood glistening darkly in the moonlight.

War Cloud said in a low, even, unalarmed voice that rang clear in the quiet night, "You all right over there, brother?"

"Better than this poor son of a bitch."

"You better come over and look at this, brother," said War Cloud.

"What's that?"

"We're rich men, Custis."

Chapter 8

Longarm saw a faint glow in the rocks off to his right, in the direction from which War Cloud's voice had come. Leaving the dead man where he lay on the cholla, he made his way across the shoulder of the slope until he was looking down into a hollow cut in the rock-strewn hillside.

In the hollow, by the low fire burning there with a coffeepot sitting inside the stone ring and on a flat rock to stay warm, War Cloud stood, looking up at Longarm. The Indian's lined face was creased with one of his dev- ilish grins.

He held his Spencer repeater out and down, indicat- ing the pair of saddlebags near the fire. Longarm knew what he'd find inside the bags even before he skipped rocks down into the hollow and flipped one of the flaps back. He stared down into the pouch stuffed with pack- ets of banded greenbacks and cream-colored burlap sacks. Longarm plucked one of the small sacks up out

of the pouch. Coins clinked inside. He hefted it in his hand.

"Gold, I'd say."

"We could head for Frisco, brother," War Cloud said. "I hear the women are pretty there." He grinned again, betraying the fact he was joshing. Longarm had never known a more honest or honorable man than War Cloud.

"Must be several thousand dollars in these bags," Longarm said, glancing into the other pouch. "That'd buy a lot of whiskey and women, all right."

"A holdup," War Cloud said. "We almost run up on a pack of curly wolves, Custis. Probably thought we were part of some posse after them."

Longarm nodded. "We'll take the money along to . . ."

He let his voice trail off as the clacking of hooves rose just south of his and War Cloud's position, and lower. He and the Apache scout walked over to stand on the lip of the cut through which the trail threaded.

Magpie was coming along the trail on her buckskin, trailing War Cloud's grulla and Longarm's dun by the horses' reins. She held one of her revolvers in the same hand in which she held her own reins and brought the buckskin to a sudden halt when her wary gaze found her father and Longarm standing over her.

War Cloud told the girl in Apache that all was well and for her to bring the horses over to where the outlaws' three mounts were picketed in some mesquites farther down the slope. Then Longarm and War Cloud started to turn back to the campfire. They both stopped and turned back to the cut at the same time, neither saying anything as they stood quietly, pricking their ears.

From farther off along the trail, on the other side of

the cut through the razorback ridge, the clamor of many hooves rose. A good-sized band of riders was heading toward the cut.

Longarm and War Cloud shared a look.

The Indian said, "More curly wolves, maybe, eh?"

"Maybe. Or the posse after them." Longarm started leaping boulders as he dropped down into the cut. "Only one way to find out."

He leaped from the last boulder to the trail. War Cloud followed him down. The two men jogged back along the cut through the ridge, the high walls rising around them to block out the moon and the stars. Ahead, the rataplan of the oncoming riders grew quickly.

War Cloud and Longarm did not have to speak to know the other's intentions. They'd worked together enough in the past and, while belonging to separate races, were cut enough from the same cloth to know instinctively how to work together without a lot of chinning about it.

As they left the cut and walked out onto the flat, Longarm moved off the trail's left side while War Cloud slipped off to the right. Longarm dropped down behind a twisted mesquite, and doffed his hat to make his shadow smaller. The pearl light of dawn was beginning to leech into the sky, making both him and War Cloud easier to see. On the other side of the trail, War Cloud crouched behind a boulder, holding his Spencer repeater up high across his chest.

The drumming of the riders' hooves continued. Staring along his back trail, Longarm saw the shifting shadows as the group drew closer. Even with the gradually intensifying dawn light, it was impossible to see how

many riders were along the trail. They were a shifting,
gray-purple mass as they approached Longarm and War
Cloud, and the cut just beyond.

Longarm didn't so much as see or hear as he sensed
movement behind him. He glanced over his left shoulder
to see Magpie move stealthily off the trail, to pass
behind him and drop down behind another mesquite to
his left. The girl hadn't made a sound. She had not
looked at Longarm as she slipped away from the trail,
and she did not look at him now.

An odd one, that girl. But while she rarely made eye
contact with Longarm, he sensed that she was keeping
an eye on him, just the same . . .

Puzzling.

Longarm gave his attention to the trail. He frowned.
The clomping of the hooves had stopped about sixty
yards away. He could see the clumped riders as a vague,
purple mass. The group had probably heard the gunfire.
Whoever they were, they were wisely wary.

As the sun continued to rise toward the horizon and
more light bled into the eastern sky, he could make out
what he thought was gold trim on the blue hat of the
lead rider. Also, farther back in the group what appeared
to be a guidon buffeted gently.

A company flag?

Longarm glanced at War Cloud. The scout glanced
back at him. Silently, they agreed to hold their
positions.

Voices sounded in conferring tones. Then one of the
group separated from the others and came on ahead on
what appeared an army bay. The lone rider came on
slowly, hooves thudding softly in the well-churned dust

of the trail. When Longarm made out the sergeant's chevrons on the sleeves of the soldier's blue tunic, the lawman rose to stand beside the mesquite while War Cloud and Magpie held their positions.

"That's far enough, Sergeant," Longarm said.

The soldier reined his bay up sharply about twenty yards back along the trail. The man's startled horse side-stepped and blew, rippling its withers and shaking its head.

The man in the saddle was burly. He wore a leather-billed forage hat and suspenders over his blue cavalry tunic.

The lawman could see the man's eyes flash wildly beneath the brim of his cap. Just as the sergeant began to lower the carbine he'd been holding barrel up on a stout thigh, Longarm said, "Easy, soldier. I'm a deputy United States marshal. The men you're after are dead and the loot is secure."

Longarm set his rifle on his shoulder, making no quick movements in case the sergeant was trigger-happy, and stepped out onto the trail. "If it's them you're after, I mean," he added.

The sergeant looked at him askance and flexed his yellow-gloved hand around the neck of his army-issue Spencer repeater. "We're after three yellow-bellied scalawags, true enough," the man said in a deep, slightly raspy voice. "But how do I know you ain't . . . ?"

"Is that ole Tom Fitzpatrick I hear bellyachin' up there on that army bay, Custis?" War Cloud stepped out onto the trail, his own Spencer repeater resting on his shoulder.

Longarm glanced at the scout, who looked up at the

sergeant, white teeth showing between his parted, upswept lips.

"Well, jumpin' Jehoshaphat," sputtered the sergeant, who appeared to be in his late thirties, early forties. "If it ain't that old dog eater, War Cloud his own mangy self!"

The sergeant hipped around in his saddle and bellowed at the group behind him, "Come on in, Captain! It's all clear—got us a federal lawman and an old friend here!"

The sergeant reached forward to shove his carbine into its saddle boot and then crawled heavily out of the saddle. He walked up to War Cloud, grinning broadly, and pumping the Indian's outstretched hand. "Good to see you, kid. What in the hell brings you back to this next of the woods, and how in the hell did you run down them curly wolves for us? Two days ago they robbed the stage out of Tombstone, an' we finally cut their trail yesterday afternoon."

Fitzpatrick's eyes widened. He shifted his gaze between Longarm and War Cloud, and then pointed at both men, saying, "Oh, wait a minute. By thunder, I bet you're both here to . . ." He let his voice trail off, and then, as the rest of his patrol rode on up behind him, he shielded his mouth with his left hand as he whispered, "Not to speak of it in front of the enlisted men. Just the captain."

The sergeant shook his head darkly, emphasizing that the subject shouldn't be blabbered out.

"What do we have here, Sergeant?" asked the lead rider, a rangy, mustached young man with captain's bars on the shoulders of his dark blue uniform blouse.

He frowned beneath the brim of his blue kepi whose left side brim was pinned up against the crown. There were seven other soldiers, including the guidon bearer, riding behind him. All the bays were sweat-silvered and dusty and weary-looking. They'd obviously been pushed hard for many miles.

Fitzpatrick said, "Captain Gavin Kilroy, this here rock worshiper is my old friend, War Cloud. Apache scout. You and the rest of these men wouldn't remember him, as you wasn't stationed at Fort McHenry when he was, but he served about as heroically as any soldier I've ever known."

The sergeant turned to Longarm, and his gaze became uncertain. "And this here man is a federal deputy marshal."

"Deputy U.S. Marshal Custis P. Long, at your service, Captain," Longarm said, reaching up to shake the hand of the young officer. "I, too, am a friend of War Cloud's. Friend and colleague. We worked together several times back when he was tracking for the U.S. marshals. We were heading for McHenry on official business when we were bushwhacked . . . by the very three stage robbers you boys are after, I understand."

Most folks would have given War Cloud two or three skeptical looks. Not the young captain. There was probably a whole stable of Apache scouts at Fort McHenry, there being no more valuable tool for tracking Apaches than other Apaches.

"Pleased to meet both you gentlemen," he said. "Are you sure you got the men we're aft . . . ?"

The captain let his voice trail off when Magpie stepped soundlessly onto the trail behind Longarm and

her father. The girl stood with her moccasins spread, thumbs hooked behind her shell belt, staring with that typically skeptical glower.

The sergeant and the captain had both jerked slightly with starts and touched their guns. But now the captain, scrutinizing the girl though he probably couldn't see much of her in the misty near-dawn light, said, "And who is this?"

War Cloud introduced his daughter.

Fitzpatrick said in shock, "That . . . that there full-growed miss is your little Magpie?"

"She sure is," War Cloud crowed.

"Why, last time I seen her—and it wasn't all that long ago—she was only hock-high to a deer tick! Look at her now!"

Fitzpatrick stepped forward, eyes bright with an older man's joy at seeing a child again he hadn't seen in years. Magpie's face remained hard as sand-scoured granite, long, dark eyes reflecting the growing light.

"Hey there, you little tadpole—you remember me? Why, sure you do. You were probably six, seven years old last time I . . ."

Fitzpatrick stopped, frowned, as the girl said something in Coyotero to her father, almost barking the guttural words, before swinging around and taking long strides along the cut toward where they'd left the stolen money and the horses.

"Don't mind her, Sergeant," Longarm said. "That's practically a bear hug compared to the greeting I got from the girl!"

Chapter 9

"It would be best, Marshal Long," said Captain Kilroy as they rode along in the early morning sunshine toward Fort McHenry, "if you keep the real reason you and War Cloud have come to McHenry under your hat."

The captain's long-legged bay blew and twitched its ears to the right of Longarm, both men and War Cloud leading up the south-heading contingent.

"Could you chew that up a little finer for me, Captain? Sergeant Fitzpatrick mentioned it when we first met, but I find it hard to believe none of the enlisted men are aware of what happened."

"Oh, there are plenty of rumors going around, of course, but I and the four other officers at McHenry have done our best to quash them. The men are not to speak of the . . . uh . . . the *incident*. You see, Major Belcher is somewhat thin-skinned on the subject, as I'm sure you can imagine anyone might be. Finding out that your wife was . . . is . . . carrying on . . ."

"With an Injun," War Cloud finished the thought for the captain.

The scout rode on the other side of the captain from Longarm. Magpie rode behind her father, with Sergeant Fitzpatrick. The rest of the patrol followed from about thirty yards behind, well out of hearing, especially with the B Company guidon buffeting in the hot, dry breeze, and with the horses clomping and snorting in the growing desert heat.

A couple of the privates were trailing the three outlaws' dead horses, with the dead outlaws themselves strapped belly down across their saddles. Sergeant Fitzpatrick had the saddlebags containing the stage loot draped securely across his own horse's withers.

Kilroy glanced at War Cloud. "I'm sure that does indeed make it worse. Of course, it shouldn't—the color of a man's skin shouldn't matter—but we all know that it does. Especially out here, with the Apache Wars just now beginning to wind down. The major is a proud man. His wife has run off with an Apache scout. I don't think it's even completely sunk in yet what has happened. At first, he believed, or wanted to believe, that Black Twisted Pine had taken Mrs. Belcher against her will. But then, one of the other officer's wives informed Major Belcher that her fleeing with the Apache scout had been something that Mrs. Belcher had been planning for several weeks in advance. According to Mrs. Pritchard—that's Captain Dwayne Pritchard's wife— Mrs. Belcher had fallen quite deeply in love with Black Twisted Pine."

"I'm sure that was something the major wanted to hear," Longarm said, ironically, biting off the end of a

three-for-a-nickel cheroot. "Hope he didn't kill the messenger."

"I think it must have been something he suspected—deep down. I have it on good word from my own wife that Mrs. Pritchard shared the information with the major not to hurt him further but only because she didn't want him going after the couple and possibly killing Black Twisted Pine. She wanted the major to know that his wife had not been abducted."

"Sounds like Mrs. Pritchard is sympathetic to Mrs. Belcher and Black Twisted Pine," Longarm said, cupping a match to the end of his cheroot.

The captain nodded as he stared gravely along the trail. "She is, indeed." He glanced at Longarm. "She thinks they should be left alone. She seems to believe that Lucy . . . er, Mrs. Belcher . . . will be happier in the Shadow Montañas with Black Twisted Pine than she has been with the major."

The captain had said all this in a neutral tone. Aside from using the major's wife's first name, that was. It was hard to tell how the young officer really felt about all this—Major Belcher, Mrs. Belcher, Black Twisted Pine, and the latter two running off together. Since the group still had a few miles left to ride before they'd reach Fort McHenry, Longarm decided to do a little probing. He didn't know what information he might get out of the man that might help him to both track and understand his quarry.

"Tell me about Mrs. Belcher—will you, Captain?"

The captain sighed and looked around, brushing at a blackfly buzzing around his thick, black dragoon mustache that bore not a hint of gray. Longarm thought he was probably still in his middle twenties.

"What's to say about her? My wife and I have had dinner several times with the Belchers, as we all take turns having the other officers over to our separate quarters. Not much to do out here when we're not chasing hostiles. It's a lonely place."

"But about Mrs. Belcher . . ." Longarm urged, frowning at the captain as he puffed his cigar. He was a little puzzled by the man's reluctance to talk about the woman.

"Mrs. Belcher is . . ." The captain stared straight ahead over his horse's ears as he swayed easily on his McClellan saddle. He seemed to be trying to find the exact words. "She is a beautiful painting of a delicate flower."

The captain continued to stare off for a few seconds before turning to Longarm and then blushing, as though suddenly embarrassed. He glanced to his other side, at War Cloud, who was studying the captain with probably much the same, vaguely incredulous expression as Longarm.

Kilroy then glanced behind him, as though wondering if the sergeant or any of the other men had heard him, and then he turned forward again in his saddle.

"What I'm saying is, Marshal Long—Mrs. Belcher is a beautiful woman. It's no big secret. Everyone knows it's true."

Longarm glanced across the captain's horse's bobbing head at War Cloud, who returned the look, slightly hiking his left shoulder.

"And the major . . . ?" Longarm asked.

"Well, I reckon you'll see for yourself soon," Kilroy said as they followed the trail to the top of a low hill.

Beyond, along the near side of a dry wash, lay the adobe-brick buildings, brush jacales, and cottonwood stables of Fort McHenry. "There it is now. You'll also be able to see for yourself just what Mrs. Belcher is like."

Longarm arched a puzzled brow.

The captain glanced at Longarm, cocking an oblique grin. "Mrs. Belcher's twin sister, Leslie, is visiting. She came down from Prescott after her sister ran off, and she's been here ever since, waiting to receive Mrs. Belcher when she returns."

As the horses started down the hill toward the sorry-looking fort nestled on a flat stretch of sage- and cactus-stippled ground, hemmed in all sides by rocky hills in addition to a tabletop mesa in the north, the young captain shook his head as though in appreciation for the images floating around just behind his eyes. "Spittin' image, Miss Leslie is. The spittin' image of her sister. They're twins, don't you know."

"Twins," Longarm said, half to himself. "No kiddin'."

"She's staying with me and my wife. Wouldn't be right, of course, to have her rooming with the major without another woman around."

"Of course not."

At the bottom of the hill, Longarm's horse pricked its ears and gave a whinny. A couple of the other mounts beside him did the same, as they were probably smelling the fresh water and hay likely emanating from one of the large barns standing on the far side of the fort, where a small herd of cattle crazed the sparse brown grass. Longarm and the others followed the trail past a brush arbor guardhouse set up beneath a large cottonwood where two privates stood on guard duty.

Both privates stood at attention and saluted as Kilroy rode past, their incredulous gazes raking the strangers, eyes narrowing curiously at the girl who didn't so much as offer them a passing glance.

There was no stockade around McHenry, but Longarm could see a couple of Gatling guns set up on knolls around the side of the fort facing the wash from which any attack from one of the roaming bands of hostiles was most likely to come. The guns were tended by two soldiers each, sheltered from the unforgiving sun by lean-to tents that flapped in the wind and flashed in the sun.

The patrol stopped where the trail curved off to the west of the parade ground, near the sutler's store and the enlisted men's barracks.

Kilroy glanced at Longarm, "Shall we see the commander, Marshal? I'm sure you'd all like to freshen up, but Major Belcher has been rather antsy for you to get here . . . since he hasn't been allowed to go after his wife himself."

"Why not?" Longarm said, swinging down from his saddle.

Out of habit, he shucked his Winchester from his saddle boot and set it on his arm. As War Cloud and Magpie dismounted, Longarm looked around at the mud-brick buildings surrounding the parade ground.

Morning drills were over; the parade ground itself was nearly vacant. It was a dry flat scored with the marks of thousands of boots and spurs. The flag standing in the center of it flapped and flashed in the wind and sun. One soldier in a battered tan kepi was pushing a wheelbarrow slowly around, stopping to shovel horseshit.

Soldiers, looking too young to be here, lounged

around out front of the enlisted men's barracks, half out of uniform. They owned the weary, bored expressions of most of the other soldiers Longarm had seen stationed at remote outposts for months on end. When boredom and frustration didn't plague these men, the threat of bloody, possibly slow, excruciating death, often did.

"How's it feel to be back on an army outpost?" Longarm asked War Cloud, who stood beside the federal lawman, casting his gaze slowly around the buildings encircling the parade ground.

"It feels good. It feels like home. I wouldn't want to live here again permanent-like, Custis, but you know I am a warrior, like all Apaches. And being around other warriors feels like the right place for me."

He glanced at Magpie standing off his right shoulder and asked the girl in Coyotero if she remembered the place. She looked around, pursed her lips, arched her brows, and hiked her shoulders with indifference.

It was an odd gesture for a young Apache woman, one that told Longarm that more of the White Eyes' culture had rubbed off on her than she probably would have admitted. Or maybe more than she was consciously aware of.

"Shall we, gentlemen . . . and . . . Miss Magpie?" Kilroy slung the saddlebags containing the stolen stagecoach money over his shoulder and gestured toward a low, brush-roofed adobe on the opposite side of the parade ground, sandwiched between the fort barber shop and the officers' and noncommissioned officers' barracks. The low shack bore a plank attached to a post near the steps leading up onto a narrow stoop, and the plank had the words FORT COMMANDER burned into it.

While a trooper led their horses off toward the stables at the rear of the camp, Captain Kilroy and the fort's visitors tramped across the parade ground, lifting little puffs of dust with every step. Longarm followed the captain up the gray wooden steps, flanked by War Cloud and Magpie. The captain knocked once on the half-open door, called, "Major Belcher, visitors to see you, sir."

The captain received no reply, but he pushed the door wide and walked inside the office bearing a desk much too large for the small space. Longarm had heard the clattering from the porch, and it was louder now as he doffed his hat and walked into the room to stand beside the captain, on the other side of the commanding officer's messy desk. The desk was flanked by a large, framed map of southern Arizona Territory and northern Mexican Sonora.

The clattering continued to emanate through a door that stood six-inches open, behind and right of the commanding officer's desk. It sounded as though someone were pounding a hammer.

But then Longarm heard the guttural growls and groans and, being no stranger to such sounds himself, recognized them even before, canting his head slightly to one side, he peered into the room beyond the door.

It was a small bedroom. Longarm could see part of a bed and a dresser to the right of the bed's foot. A brown-skinned girl was leaning forward against the dresser, standing sideways to Longarm. She was completely naked. A yellow dress lay crumpled around her delicate, brown, bare feet.

The girl leaned into her outstretched arms, hand clasping the front side of the dresser. What was making

the hammering sounds was the dresser being smacked against the wall as someone rammed the girl from behind. Her cherry-tan, brown-tipped breasts bounced sharply with each smashing thrust.

Chapter 10

Longarm couldn't see the man fucking the girl. Only the girl herself.

As the man continued fucking her, she turned toward Longarm. Her chocolate-brown eyes flicked across the lawman and Captain Kilroy before she turned her head forward again and squeezed her eyes closed, wincing against the violent thrusts.

"Good Christ," Kilroy muttered and walked around behind the desk. He held the door's latch with one hand, knocked on the door once with his other hand, and turned discreetly back toward Longarm. "Major—you have visitors," the captain said, louder this time.

"Ah, hell!" grunted the man inside the room.

Kilroy pulled the door closed, sighed, and then, not meeting Longarm's or War Cloud's gaze—Magpie remained in the office's open doorway—walked back out from behind the desk.

The door opened a foot. A haggard, bearded face and

one pale blue eye peered out the crack. *"Fuck!"* the man cried miserably and slammed the door.

From inside the room came thud slaps of bare feet stomping, stumbling around the room, making the floor beneath Longarm's boots quiver.

"That's Major Belcher?" Longarm asked Kilroy, his tone ironic.

"Yes, it's Major Belcher. He's not like this, Marshal. You have to understand."

"He's heartsick."

"Yes." As though realizing how ridiculous his reply must have sounded, he glanced at Longarm sheepishly, flushing. "He's really not like this. For Christ's sake— the man's wife ran off with an Apache scout."

Longarm glanced at War Cloud, who stood back by the door, near his daughter. Both the Indians were stone-faced. War Cloud met Longarm's glance and shrugged, a humorous light glinting in his right eye.

Behind the door, Belcher muttered under his breath as he stomped around, grunting and clearing his throat, apparently dressing.

"Go on—get out of here," he growled loudly enough for Longarm to hear him through the door.

The door opened a couple of feet. The Apache girl stood in the opening. She wore a frilly yellow dress— obviously a young white woman's expensive party dress. Something she'd wear to a summer dance.

It looked ridiculous on the brown-skinned girl who owned the pretty but raw features of a full-blood Apache. The dress had no sleeves and only rose about halfway up her breasts. The girl's badly mussed, coarse,

blue-black hair hung down past her shoulders. Strands stood out around her head like black wires.

"Go on, Blue Feather," Kilroy said, tossing his arm toward the office door.

The girl drew the door open wider and hurried out, leaving the door partly open behind her. She scampered barefoot out from behind the desk and, keeping her head down, one hand clamped across her mouth, nearly ran past War Cloud and Magpie and outside.

Longarm heard her bare feet pad across the porch and then thump down onto the ground. Her running footsteps dwindling quickly into the distance.

Kilroy leaned toward Longarm and said under his breath, "Warm Springs Apache," as though that explained something. "Orphan. Works on suds row, performs other . . . odd jobs around the fort."

Suds row was where the laundry of the fort was washed by a small contingent of women who lived on or around the fort, including Native girls and noncommissioned officers' wives.

The door opened sharply and the man whom Longarm took to be Major Belcher stood in the opening, tucking his shirttails into his pants. "What was that, Captain?" He glared angrily, suspiciously.

Captain Kilroy regarded him dubiously. "I just mentioned that Blue Feather is a Warm Springs Apache, Anson. That's all." He cleared his throat. "These are the men we've been waiting for—Deputy U.S. Marshal Custis Long and a man who apparently scouted here at McHenry some time ago—War Cloud. He's a Coyotero."

Belcher studied the men critically. He was a large,

handsome man around thirty, Longarm judged, though the lines around his eyes and soft waistline made him look older. His eyes were cold and arrogant.

He had thick, dark brown hair parted in the middle and hanging long over his ears, brushing the collar of his bib-front blue cavalry blouse. The whites of his blue eyes were a network of bright red lines. They were rheumy from drink. He seemed to have trouble focusing.

Lowering his gaze now with apparent chagrin— something told Longarm that it was not a common emotion for him—he buttoned his fly, slid his suspender up over his broad shoulders, and came on into the room.

"Warm Springs Apache, yes." Belcher sagged into his swivel chair, which squawked and creaked beneath his weight. He lounged back negligently, wrists dangling over the chair's arms. "Blue Feather. Sorry, gentlemen— I don't reckon that looked too professional. But we're not all that fixed on form around here. What man doesn't have a dalliance once in a while?"

He glanced at first Longarm and then War Cloud. His eyes strayed to Magpie standing against the door, arms crossed on her breasts.

"Say, what we got there?"

"That's War Cloud's daughter," Longarm said before War Cloud could say anything.

The lawman sensed the acrimony building in the Coyotero scout, and he didn't want to kick things off here at Fort McHenry on the wrong foot. He couldn't help adding, however, "Her father's right protective of the girl, though I've seen how she can handle herself right fine."

Belcher let his half-drunk gaze linger on the girl for a few more seconds and, as though Longarm's words had taken a while to register, switched his gaze to the tall federal lawman standing between Kilroy and War Cloud. Belcher wrinkled the skin above the bridge of his nose.

"Don't talk crap to me, federal boy," he said, lines of anger cutting across his pale forehead.

Longarm drew a short breath to stem the rising tide of his own anger. He kept his voice almost ridiculously mild as he said, "I wasn't talking crap to you, Major. I was simply telling you how it was, that's all."

"You don't like me—I can see that already."

"Anson," Kilroy said.

"Shut up, Captain. Don't speak until you're spoken to." The major rubbed a finger across the brass oak leaves on his left shoulder and then cast his bleary gaze at Longarm once more. "You don't think I should be . . . uh . . . entertaining at such a time, so you've already made up your mind about me. Isn't that it, Marshal Long?"

Longarm said nothing.

"You show me a soldier who doesn't entertain outside the marriage once in a while, and I'll show you a stuffed uniform who knows nothing about life in this neck of the woods. Just because I fuck an Apache washer girl once in a while to ease the nerves of commanding a fort out here in the high and rocky don't mean I don't love my wife and want her back. It don't mean that goddamn redskin had any right to cart her away from me in the middle of the fuckin' night!"

Uncharacteristically showing his emotion, War Cloud

said, "I heard she wasn't carted away. She went willingly. My friend Black Twisted Pine wouldn't take a woman against her will. No Apache would. To do so would be to dishonor himself as well as his family!"

"Who told you she went *willingly*?" Kilroy slapped the desk.

Kilroy said defensively, "They would have found out sooner or later, Anson. They *needed* to know!"

Longarm said, "Hell, even Washington knows that. What Captain Kilroy told me wasn't news."

Kilroy was sitting up straight in his chair now, glaring at the captain. "Don't call me by my first name, Captain. We're not having drinks and playing cards over at the sutler's store. We're on duty here."

Kilroy drew a breath and looked at the floor. "I'm sorry . . . Major Belcher."

The major glared at Longarm and then at War Cloud. He grabbed a pack of ready-made cigars off his desktop that was a mess of ledger books and duty rosters. The cigars were in a red foil package with *Season's Greetings* written in gold cursive script across the top. Beneath an oval picture of a beautiful woman in Egyptian headgear was the label *Anthony y Cleopatra: The Mildest Havana Cigar.*

A gift from last Christmas, Longarm surmised. Probably sent by one of the major's moneyed relatives from back East. One pack of many, most likely.

The major plucked a small, perfectly rolled, coffee-brown cigarillo from the pack. He scratched a match to life on the desktop, lit the cigarillo, and puffed smoke at his guests.

"I want her brought back to me, Marshal," he sat back

in his chair again. "I want them both brought back to
me. I'll deal with Mrs. Belcher in my own way. I'll deal
with that"—he glanced at War Cloud and quirked his
mouth corners devilishly—"that *savage* in my own way,
as well."

Longarm glanced at War Cloud, ready to grab the
scout if he needed to. He was relieved to see that War
Cloud had a firm hold on himself. He merely lifted his
chin slightly and scowled down his nose at the drunken
major.

"That kind of an attitude ain't gonna get us anywhere," Longarm said. "Our orders are to ride down
south of the border, track your wife and Black Twisted
Pine down, and convince Mrs. Belcher to come back up
here to Fort McHenry with us. We're not on any assas-
sination mission. As far as I've been told, and as far as
what I read in the file on the way down here, Black
Twisted Pine isn't bein' accused of a crime."

"You look here, goddamnit, Marshal!" Belcher
climbed out of his chair as quickly as he could in his
inebriated state and flicked his cigar at Longarm. The
cigarillo bounced off Longarm's vest and sparked to
the floor at his boots.

Those sparks kindled a fire not too deep inside the
federal lawman. He felt forking veins bulge in his
forehead.

"I'm giving the orders around here! You see? I've
minded my manners and followed the orders sent out
from Washington not to track my wife and that dog eater
into the Shadow Montañas. I've been waiting for you to
do it. Now that you're here—that's exactly what you're
gonna do. And you're gonna haul them both back to me.

And if you don't, I'll ride out with every able-bodied man at this outpost . . . and a wagon outfitted with Gatling guns . . . and I'll do the job myself!"

Longarm drew a ragged breath. Grinding his back teeth together, he leaned forward over the major's desk and said in a calm, even voice that belied his fury, "You listen to me, *Major* Belcher. You're not giving the orders. Neither I nor War Cloud are under your command. We're here by order of the chief marshal of Denver's First District, and we answer to him and only to him.

"As far as I can tell, you're nothin' more than a drunk and lecher far too big for your britches. You probably don't deserve that woman of yours back in the first place. But just to keep the peace around here, that's what me and War Cloud are gonna do. Black Twisted Pine will be free to go his own way."

Belcher had been staring up in raw, red-faced fury at the federal lawman. Suddenly, he leaped up out of his chair and ran around from behind it.

Kilroy got in front of him, blocking his way. "Anson, no!"

Kilroy got a resolute right fist to his jaw for his efforts. The captain grunted and flew back against the office's front wall, knocking a picture off a nail.

Belcher turned to Longarm, bringing a haymaker up from his heels. Ready for it, Longarm raised his left arm to shield his own face, and punched the major twice in the jaw and cheek with more force than was prudent. The way Longarm saw it, the man had had it coming back when he'd so rudely disposed of his cigar.

Belcher stumbled backward, arms flopping, eyelids

fluttering. He was out before he hit the floor in front of the door behind which he'd been fucking the Apache girl.

"Ah, shit," Longarm said, waving his aching fist in the air.

"Yeah, that didn't go too good, brother," said War Cloud.

Magpie was peering over her father's shoulder at the fallen major.

Longarm helped Kilroy to his feet. Blood dribbled from the young captain's split lower lip.

"You all right, Captain?" Longarm asked the lad.

Kilroy nodded. "I think so." He shook his head, staring down at the fort's unconscious commanding officer. "Well . . ." He gave a wry chuckle. "Welcome to Fort McHenry, gentlemen."

Chapter 11

Kilroy seemed to feel genuinely bad about the dustup in Major Belcher's office. He said it would probably be best if he put the major to bed and gave him time to sober up before they "visited" further. He assured the visitors that the incident in the office was out of character for the normally more restrained camp commander.

The poor man just had his neck up over his missing wife.

Kilroy arranged for Longarm and War Cloud to throw down in a vacant unmarried officers' quarters, the row of which sat beside the fort sutler's store that had a small, lean-to saloon attached. Through the major's adjutant, Corporal Carson, the captain arranged for Magpie to stay with one of the noncommissioned officer's families, though when War Cloud explained this to Magpie, the girl spat out in her guttural tongue that she'd rather sleep in a dry wash with bobcats.

With a tense smile, War Cloud assured the captain
that his daughter was grateful for the amenities. Then
he gave his strident young princess a blank, subtly commanding stare. While the girl was led away by the non-
com's merry, full-hipped wife, Longarm and War Cloud
followed Corporal Carson over to the row of unmarried
officer's quarters.

War Cloud and Longarm had a quick drink and a
short nap. War Cloud was out of sorts. He got up in the
early afternoon and headed off to pay a visit to the three
other Apache scouts stationed at McHenry.

He wanted to confer with them about Black Twisted
Pine and to generally "get the lay of the land around
here." The corporal had informed him that the scouts'
quarters were still back near the barn and stables, at the
base of the tabletop mesa rising north of the parade
ground.

Longarm himself wanted to consult with the scouts
but knew that War Cloud would probably gather more
information about the Apaches' point of view without
a white man present. Especially a white federal
lawman.

He bit off the end of a cigar and headed on out of the
pent-up heat in his room to sit on a bench under the
brush-roofed ramada facing the parade ground and
smoke his cigar, sip from his bottle of Tom Moore, and
gather some wool on the situation at hand.

The fort was quiet in the afternoon. The only sounds
were a few soldiers talking in the saloon attached to the
sutler's store to Longarm's right, the occasional whinny
of a horse out in one of the corrals, and the rumble of
thunder in a purple storm mass sliding over the northern

mesa. The air shepherded along in front of the storm was cool and refreshing as it blew against Longarm's face.

It smelled of desert sage and rain.

Longarm closed his eyes and let the cool, fragrant wind brush against him as he smoked the cigar and registered beneath the growing rumble of the oncoming storm the thunder of discontent in his own mind.

What in hell were he and War Cloud doing down here, anyway? It was looking more and more like they'd been sent by the federal government to fetch a woman back to a pathetic lout of a husband. A man whom Longarm had witnessed banging a young Apache girl in his office.

To fetch the woman back, against her will, from the man she apparently really loved.

And the poor woman's husband wanted Longarm and War Cloud to haul Black Twisted Pine back to McHenry, as well, so that Belcher could punish the man in his own likely devious and savage way. Longarm had to assume that if Belcher got his hands on his cuckolder, he'd kill Black Twisted Pine.

His grim ruminations were mercifully cut short when he spied Corporal Carson leading a small troop of privates across the parade ground from the direction of the bathhouse. The corporal—a lanky, towheaded lad who seemed to perpetually be smiling—was carrying a copper bathtub while the two privates each carried two steaming buckets, wincing and grunting with the effort.

"A bath for you, sir—ordered by Major Belcher!" intoned Corporal Carson as he mounted the gallery, beaming.

Longarm flicked his cigar stub into the dirt as the privates followed the corporal into his room, their boots drumming on the dry puncheons. "Belcher? You mean Kilroy."

The clank of the tub being set down inside issued from the open door. Presently, Carson stuck his head out to say, "No, sir. Apparently, the major sobered up and realized he'd made a mistake. He's been sort of off his feed since his wife left to visit her family back East."

Carson had slightly emphasized that last sentence, and he gave Longarm an ironic wink. Apparently, that had been the explanation the enlisted men had been given for Mrs. Belcher's disappearance although, obviously, Carson knew the truth. As likely did the rest of the soldiers at Fort McHenry.

"I'm sure it was nothing personal," Carson explained. "Anyway, he ordered a bath of hot water sent over from the bathhouse, so that you may bathe in private, sir. He also ordered me to invite you and War Cloud and the young . . . um . . . lady—Miss Magpie, wasn't it?—to his private residence for supper with him and Mrs. Belcher's sister, Miss Leslie, this evening at six o'clock. The major wants very much to give you a proper sendoff."

"Well, I'll be," Longarm said, wary of the major's intentions. He didn't trust the man any farther than he could throw him uphill against a Dakota twister. What the man had said while drunk this afternoon concerning the trouble at hand was probably much closer to the truth than anything he'd say sober this evening.

As the privates exited Longarm's quarters with their empty buckets and started walking back in the direction

of the bathhouse, Corporal Carson said, "Can I inform the major you'll accept his offer?"

"Sure, why not?" Longarm said, shrugging. He had to eat somewhere. And he wouldn't mind meeting the major's sister-in-law, whom Kilroy had informed him was the major's wife's twin. At least he'd have a description of the gal he and War Cloud would be looking for.

"Wonderful! It's that house at the east end of the parade ground. Enjoy your bath, Marshal! I set a brush and some soap on the table, as well as a bottle of brandy compliments of the major!"

With that, the Corporal saluted out of habit. Longarm awkwardly returned the gesture from his chair and watched the corporal step down off the gallery and head across the parade ground. He was striding in the direction of the narrow, two-story house he'd pointed out— one of three plain, neat, shake-shingled dwellings that sat in a row at the parade ground's east end, behind a picket fence in badly need of fresh paint.

"Brandy, eh?"

Longarm heaved his travel-weary bones out of the chair and went inside his borrowed quarters. Sure enough, a bottle of brandy sat on the small pine desk opposite the bunk bed. Not just any brandy, either. Spanish brandy.

Longarm popped the cork, sniffed.

Expensive stuff. Nothing he'd ever tasted equaled his favored Tom Moore, but he wouldn't turn down a bottle of Spanish brandy. The corporal had provided a goblet.

Longarm filled the glass to the brim and spilled a little when thunder peeled, giving him a start. He corked

the bottle and started to remove his string tie as he peered out one of the room's two windows curtained with what appeared old cavalry tunics. Nothing went to waste on a remote cavalry outpost.

The swollen purple clouds were nearly straight over the parade ground, dragging along a pale curtain of rain. As lightning flashed wickedly against the purple, anvil-shaped mass, thunder cracked sharply. Raindrops flecked against the sashed window.

The desert rain tempered Longarm's dread of the grim situation at hand. There was nothing quite as refreshing as rain in the desert—especially rain in the middle of an especially hot desert summer. And he had a hot bath and a bottle of brandy to go along with it.

He got undressed and tossed his clothes onto the hide-bottom chair behind the desk, dropping his hat down on top of the pile. He coiled his cartridge belt around his holstered six-shooter, set that on the chair, and dragged the chair near the tub, so the gun would be in easy reach in case he needed it. A lawman never knew.

He set his glass of brandy, soap, and brush on the floor near the tub and climbed into the steaming water, groaning in delight as his extra layer of skin, which consisted of over a week's worth of trail grime, began to soften. He sank all the way down in the water, dunking his head, and came up blowing.

Immediately, he climbed to his feet, lathered the brush that the corporal had provided, and began scrubbing in earnest to the storm's raucous symphony, with lightning flashing in the windows.

When he'd scraped the crud off every inch of his big,

brawny frame and even dug some chunks of dirty wax out of his ears, he lifted the one remaining bucket of water, provided for rinsing, above his head. He froze, looked at the rain-splattered window right of the door.

He'd seen something move in a corner of it. Probably only a tumbleweed blowing past in the wind. He glanced at his pistol, comforted by the nearness of the trusty popper.

He poured the remaining bucket of water over his head.

He dropped the bucket suddenly and, while the rinse water was still dribbling off his shoulders and down his chest, he reached over and grabbed his .44. Clicking the hammer back and aiming at the window on the left side of the door in which he'd glimpsed a face peering in at him from the lower right corner, he yelled, "Come on in out of the rain before I drill your peeping eyes through the glass!"

The face had disappeared. Standing naked in the tub, soaked hair pasted against his forehead and still dribbling water into his eyes, he blinked each eye in turn as he yelled, "Come in and face me like a man, you chicken-livered son of a bitch!"

He had no idea the peeper's intentions, but it was best to assume the worst.

Nothing except the rain moved in either window. There was no sound except the hammering moisture against the walls and ceiling and windows.

The door latch clicked. The door opened slowly on its rusty hinges. A young, redheaded woman looked in, looking sheepish. The nubs of her fine cheeks were touched with red.

She walked into the room holding a closed umbrella down low by her side, and then ran her eyes, green as amethysts, up and down the brawny frame of the man before her and quirked her lips in a devilish smile.

"Well, isn't this embarrassing," she said, chuckling naughtily. "I just got caught spying on a U.S. marshal taking a bath in the privacy of his own guest quarters. Well, well—congratulations, Leslie. You might just get court-martialed for this one."

Longarm depressed his Colt's hammer and lowered the piece. He didn't bother covering himself. He'd been seen naked by enough women—and this one had already seen him naked through the window—that he was pretty much immune to it. Besides, she didn't seem to mind.

"Miss McPherson, I presume?"

She smiled saucily, showing pretty, white teeth between her perfect lips. Her green eyes glimmered alluringly with each lightning flash out the windows behind her. "Marshal Long, I presume?"

Her eyes flicked unabashedly to his cock before returning to his eyes. "Out of Denver's First District Court? One of the two men sent to rescue my sister from that red demon up in the Shadow Montañas?"

"One and the same," Longarm said.

Since she was so free with her own gaze, he let his own eyes swallow her whole. Despite the umbrella, the rain had gotten to her. Her white blouse with its high neck, lace edges, and puffy sleeves, was pasted damply to her breasts, so that even through the blouse's cotton and the chemise beneath the blouse he could see the outline of the rich, round orbs.

As well as two pink nipples flattened against the material.

She was a tall girl, with light red hair falling in delicate, silky waves to her shoulders. Sausage curls hung down the sides of her face, brushing her long, fine jaws.

"Would you like a magnifying class?" the girl asked with more of a coquette's lighthearted jeering than honest admonishment. "You might see more that way."

"I got a good imagination."

"You must be conjuring something provocative."

Longarm glanced down past his belly. His dong was beginning to answer to the tingling that the well-turned girl had inflicted on his loins.

His condition making him self-conscious, Longarm reached over to slide his revolver back into its holster, and then he lowered himself down into the tub and now-tepid water. "Were you lookin' for shelter from the storm, Miss McPherson?" He smiled at the pretty girl. "Or you needin' a bath?"

Chapter 12

"Don't tempt me," Miss McPherson said, turning to close the door and glancing over her shoulder at Longarm. "But actually, Marshal . . ."

"Since you've seen my birthday suit an' all, you might as well call me Longarm."

"Longarm, eh?"

"You find somethin' funny about that?"

"Oh, not at all!"

She crossed her arms on her breasts and hiked a hip on the corner of the desk, to Longarm's left. From there she had a pretty good view into the tub. Her eyes were like fingers, toying with him, subtly arousing him. He was glad there were still enough soap bubbles to hide the affected organ.

"I don't find anything one bit funny about attractive men, Marshal Long."

She glanced at the handful of three-for-a-nickel

cheroots he'd laid out on the desk, and said, "Mind if I have one of your cigars here . . . Longarm?"

"Not if you'll light me one. Help yourself to the brandy, there, too. It's from your brother-in-law."

"Yes, I heard you cold-cocked him."

"You seem to approve, Miss McPherson."

She was looking around for a glass and when she didn't find one, Longarm held up his. "My lap's as clean as your average cur's."

"Thank you."

She filled the glass, took a sip, and set the glass on the desk. "My brother-in-law has been needing a beating for a long time, Longarm. No one has seemed to be up to the task . . . until now. For that I applaud you. But to the reason I'm here . . ."

She stuck one of the cheroots between her pretty teeth and struck a match on the top of the table. She lit the one cheroot, blowing smoke around her lovely head, and then lit a second one. When she had the second one going, she gave it to Longarm, letting smoke trickle out her fine, long nostrils.

"Thanks," Longarm said. He felt the cool dampness of her saliva on the cigar end, and it vaguely aroused him further. "And now to the reason you're here."

She retook her position on a corner of the desk, one leg dangling. Despite the black skirt she wore to her ankles, he could tell that her legs were fine and long. He had a brief, imagined glimpse of them wrapped around his back, and winced at the pleasant burn in his lower belly.

She stared at him obliquely, and then the corners of her mouth rose slightly, as though she'd read his mind.

"Yes, to why I'm here."

She puffed the cigar. She did not choke on the pungent smoke but turned her head and blew it out at the door. "I'd like you to ride out and fetch my sister back, Longarm. I'm sure she must have had a change of heart by now. She is a mercurial girl. But I want you to promise me that you won't force her to come if she doesn't want to. If she really wants to stay with Black Twisted Pine, she should be able to. Lucy should be able to do anything she wishes."

Longarm leaned back in the tub.

"Here," Leslie said, extending the glass of brandy to him.

He took the glass and threw back a third of it. He took one more sip. Then he gave the glass back to the young woman and took a drag off his cigar, blowing the smoke at the rain-splattered window.

"You have no doubt that your sister is in love with Black Twisted Pine?"

"Oh, I don't really know what to think. Maybe Lucy doesn't, either. She was always rather impetuous in matters of love. What I know, Longarm, is that her marriage is a bad one. The marriage was more or less arranged by our parents and Anson's parents. My father has business interests back East, and he's partners in several of those interests with Anson's father. In fact, my grandfather and great-grandfather were in concert with the grandfathers of Anson."

"Old, rich families."

"Yes."

"How would they feel about Lucy staying with Black Twisted Pine?"

"How do you think Lucy would feel about being hauled back here . . . to Anson . . . against her will? How do you think that she would feel if Anson does as he wishes and kills Black Twisted Pine? If Anson has his way, that's exactly what he'll do, you know."

Longarm rolled the cigar around between his teeth and sighed. He stared at the door, pensive. Lightning continued to flash in the windows but the thunder had become less loud. The brunt of the storm was passing.

"The major seems to have restrained himself so far," Longarm said.

"Only because none of the scouts here at McHenry can lead him into the Shadow Montañas. None of these Apaches—they're Lipans—have been there before. Their work has mostly been done in New Mexico. I'm told that one of the few scouts who can lead a patrol into those mountains is your friend, War Cloud, one of the few Coyotero trackers still around."

Longarm knew that was true. The Shadow Montañas were a sacred range, off-limits to all Apaches who hadn't gone through a sacred rite. That rite itself had rarely been practiced in the last twenty years, as the Apaches have had other, more important things on their mind. Namely, scouring the White Eyes from their homeland.

War Cloud was one of the few scouts—maybe the *only* scout still available to the U.S. Army—who could lead Longarm into that craggy, wild, mysterious range eighty miles south of the border. War Cloud had once fought the Mescaleros in those mountains, back when the two tribes were at war with one another. Back when

they'd considered each other more of an enemy than the white man.

"If you don't think your sister should be forced to return," Longarm asked Leslie, "what are you doing here?"

"I came because I'm very worried about her, and it seemed the logical place to come. I came here, also, to make sure that if she is returned, Anson doesn't harm her."

"You think he would?"

"I know he would. He's a bastard. You've seen that for yourself. Lucy has told me that he's struck her more than a few times."

"Ah, Jesus," Longarm said. No man in his right mind would hit a woman. Especially not the woman he was married to, supposed to be in love with.

"Anson's been cuckolded," Leslie continued. "He is a prideful man. And now, if you'll pardon my farm talk, Longarm, he is a very piss-burned cuckold. I don't doubt that he's capable of killing my sister."

She sipped from the brandy glass, staring at Longarm over the brim. She swallowed and then slid off the desk and dropped to her knees beside the tub.

She handed him the glass and then, staring at him with dark eroticism, slipped her hand over the side of the tub and into the water. She found his cock that, during their serious conversation, was finally minding its own business.

When the girl wrapped her hand around it, however, it began sparking instantly to life.

Longarm winced as she fondled him under the water,

sliding her face up close to his until he could feel the little puffs of her warm breath on his lips. Her own lips were perfectly shaped and cherry-pink.

"Miss Leslie, I don't mean nothin' by this," Longarm said tightly as she continued to manipulate him, "but are you and your sister as alike in . . . uh . . . temperament as you are in looks?"

"No," Leslie said softly, gazing into his eyes. "Lucy's a romantic. That's why it's such a tragedy she married such an uncouth goat as Anson Belcher. Me . . . I'm more practical. *Earthy.*"

Longarm's cock was now poking its swollen head above the water. She pumped it slowly, squeezing, running her hand over the top and down the other side.

"And if you bring my sister back and see that she is not harmed, Longarm, I'll show you just how practical I can be."

Longarm was watching her hand. His blood was rising, heating up. Her hand was soft as silk.

"Practical, did you say?"

"Practical. In other words, I know how to reward a man for his efforts . . . in the most practical way known to him."

She leaned closer, pressed her lips to his. She kissed him gently at first and then more hungrily, groaning softly and flicking her tongue into his mouth. At the same time, she pumped his cock faster.

Then, suddenly, she rose and smiled down at him.

"I'll see you at supper later, Longarm. It's been nice getting to know you."

She swung around, grabbed her umbrella off the desk, and, just like that, she was gone.

"H-hey!" Longarm growled indignantly, staring down at his throbbing cock.

An hour later, flanked by War Cloud and Magpie, Longarm rapped the wooden knocker in the shape of a lion's head against the door of the Belcher residence. Longarm was a little surprised to see the Apache girl, Blue Feather, open the door.

She was dressed in a light blue Mother Hubbard dress, and she wore a matching ribbon in her black hair. To dress like a civilized white girl was doubtlessly one of the rules of the house. Longarm wondered how Belcher reconciled the civilized attire to banging the girl in his office. Apparently, one of her duties at Fort McHenry was to serve as the Belchers' maid.

"Come," Blue Feather said, her features nearly as expressionless as Magpie's. There was a slight flush in her cherry-tan cheeks—likely from the embarrassment of knowing what Longarm and the other three visitors had witnessed earlier.

The girl turned and walked down the entryway, at the rear of which a narrow stairs rose to the second story, and into a door on the left. There was another door on the right from which the sound of a ticking clock issued.

Longarm looked through this doorway to see Leslie McPherson sitting in a carved walnut armchair near the small, brick fireplace, chin resting in the palm of one hand, a bored, sullen expression on her beautiful face. She was shaking a crossed leg nervously.

She turned toward Longarm and arched a brow. "Long time no see, Marshal."

Looking ravishing in a silk and taffeta gown of the same color as her eyes, her long, light red hair freshly brushed and glistening and partly secured behind her head in a chignon, she strode across the room and into the foyer. She wore a black silk choker adorned with an ivory cameo pin. She met Longarm's gaze and then glanced at War Cloud and Magpie.

Longarm cleared his throat. "War Cloud, Magpie, meet Miss Leslie McPherson. Miss McPherson is the sister of Mrs. Belcher."

Leslie dipped her chin cordially and smiled warmly. "How do you both do?"

"Pleased to make your acquaintance, ma'am," War Cloud said, doffing his hat and then hanging it on a wall peg.

Leslie glanced at the doorway through which Blue Feather had disappeared. "My brother-in-law doesn't stand much on ceremony, I'm afraid. I believe dinner is ready without preamble. Shall we?" She gestured toward the door.

"You first," Longarm said, pegging his snuff-brown Stetson.

As he followed Leslie into a small but well-appointed dining room, Leslie said over her shoulder just loudly enough for Longarm to hear. "Almost didn't recognize you dressed, Longarm. You clean up right well."

Longarm's cheeks warmed. "Why, thank you, ma'am."

"I hope I didn't injure anything earlier."

"Oh, I'll be fine," he said, stopping beside the girl as War Cloud and Magpie walked up to stand to his left.

A ten-foot, cloth-covered table lay before them. It

had been all set up with plates, silverware, and water glasses. From behind a curtained doorway rose the clatter of pans and the squawk of a stove door.

"I'm sure we can sit anywhere," Leslie said. "Longarm, why don't you take this end? I'll sit here. War Cloud, why don't you and Magpie sit there, to Longarm's left? Blue Feather will want to be close to the kitchen, and she'll want me to be as far away from it as possible." Leslie chuckled. "Smart girl. I'd burn the water."

Longarm looked around. "We're the only guests?"

"Yes," Leslie said as Longarm held her chair out for her and sagged into it. "Anson decided that in light of everything it might be best if our conversation be private. He didn't even want me here, but . . ."

"Nonsense, my dear, Leslie," the major said as he walked in from the foyer. "I simply didn't want to bore your pretty head with these somewhat rough-hewn affairs and trivial details."

Longarm had heard the man's footsteps growing steadily as he'd marched down from the second story. Now, freshly scrubbed, his thick, longish hair combed wet, and wearing a crisp blue, gold-embroidered shell jacket over a white linen shirt with a string tie, Major Belcher stopped beside Leslie's chair and leaned down to place a kiss on his sister-in-law's left cheek.

She turned her face away and his lips grazed her jaw.

He rose, flushing slightly, scowling down before recovering and saying, "Welcome, Marshal Long. War Cloud. Miss Magpie."

Longarm now saw the slight cut and swelling on Belcher's right cheek where Longarm had laid him out. It looked tender as hell.

Magpie, staring stonily across the table at Leslie, of course said nothing. War Cloud dipped his chin to the major and said, "Thanks for having us, Major."

"I take it you've already met my beautiful and charming sister-in-law."

Leslie rolled her eyes slightly. The major chuckled.

"Yes," Longarm said, shooting an ironic glance at Leslie, "I've had the pleasure."

"Wonderful. She's the spitting image of my wife. I'm sure that will be handy to know."

"It will at that," Longarm said.

War Cloud said, "We'll be off tomorrow. First thing."

"I was hoping you would be. I'd like my wife back as soon as possible. You have a long, rough ride ahead. You'd best eat heartily," the major said, glancing at Blue Feather entering the kitchen and carrying a large, cast-iron stew pot.

As she set the pot on the table near a basket of bread and a bowl of buttered peas, the major slacked into the chair at Longarm's opposite end of the table. Belcher rubbed his cheek as he said, "That's a strong right hook you have there, Marshal." He flexed his jaw.

"I'd like to apologize, Major," Longarm said, unable to contain his frankness. "But you had it coming."

Leslie glanced in surprise at Longarm and grinned delightedly.

"I did for a fact," Belcher admitted. "And I myself would like to apologize. I was completely out of line. Drunk on duty, and out of line. I'm terribly ashamed."

The man bowed his head. He said a quick table prayer and then nodded to Blue Feather sitting beside him. "Blue Feather will fill your bowls with her hearty and

succulent rabbit stew. This young lady has been cook-
ing for my wife and I since we came to Fort McHenry
two years ago, and I don't think I've eaten better food
in the finest New York restaurants. Quite a remarkable
feat, given what scant and often poor provisions the girl
is supplied with."

As the stew bowls were passed around the table for
Blue Feather to fill, Longarm sat in amazement at
Belcher's gall. He'd been caught screwing his young
housemaid only a few scant hours ago by Captain Kilroy, Longarm, War Cloud, and Magpie, and didn't look
one bit chagrined.

And still he wore his self-righteous indignation over
his young wife's indiscretions with Black Twisted Pine
on his sleeve!

Longarm wondered—hoped—that the man would
whistle a different tune this evening about wanting Longarm and War Cloud to haul not only his wife but her
lover back to Fort McHenry for punishment. That he'd
softened his stance on the undignified matter. If not, the
two men weren't going to get along much better than
they had earlier.

Chapter 13

Very little was said over the simple meal of stew, fresh bread, and wild peas roasted lightly in butter. As Belcher had promised, everything was delicious.

For dessert, Blue Feather served peach pie and whipped cream. The peaches were not fresh, of course—they came from airtight tins—but still the pie was just as tasty as the rest of the meal.

Blue Feather filled everyone's coffee cup for a second time—everyone except Magpie's, who apparently did not indulge in the White Eyes' drink, Longarm was not surprised to see. She drank only water.

Then, when Blue Feather had cleared the table and was busy washing dishes in the kitchen, Belcher set a bottle of brandy on the table. When Leslie, Longarm, and War Cloud had laced their coffee with the liquor, Belcher added a jigger to his own. He slid his chair a few inches back from the table and to one side, and

crossed one leg over the other. He sipped his coffee and stared down into his cup for a time.

Suddenly, he said, "Well, gentlemen, it's time I got down to brass tacks. If you talked at all to my sister-in-law, you've probably gotten a somewhat skewed perspective on the troublesome state of affairs here at McHenry. Uh . . . regarding my wife and that savage, that is."

Leslie shot a riled look at her brother-in-law. "Anson . . ."

The major waved her to silence and slid his gaze between Longarm and War Cloud. "Let me tell my side of it, Leslie. You've obviously had your say. I can tell by the expression in these men's eyes that they're somewhat perplexed."

"Perplexed?" Longrm said with a mirthless chuckle. "Yeah, I guess you could say I'm perplexed."

He stared hard at the major so that the man would know exactly what he was talking about—the man's dalliance in his office earlier with his young Apache housekeeper when he was supposed to be pining for his wife. And then Belcher's insistence on bringing both his wife and her lover back to the fort whether they wanted to come or not.

"Let me clear things up for you, Marshal Long and War Cloud." Belcher sipped his brandy-laced coffee, stared down into the cup, and chuckled as though he saw something funny there. He set the cup down and ran a hand through his hair, grinding his back against his chair with a grunt, as though massaging weary muscles.

When he was done, he drew a deep breath and

leveled a vaguely ironic gaze at Longarm. "I assure you that I am not a good man. No, far from it. But then, you already know that.

Belcher looked at Leslie, who held his gaze obstinately. The major grinned and shifted his gaze to Longarm and War Cloud again.

"Be that as it may, I can also assure you that I love my wife. And that she, despite the fact that she's run off with that . . . that Black Twisted Pine . . . still loves me."

"Then how can you explain what's happened?" Longarm wanted to know.

"My wife is a frail creature. Not so much in body but in mind. And, just like her sister here, she is amazingly beautiful. You can see how she would be an easy target for a strong man. A strong, lustful man. You see, she tends to romanticize the savages."

He glanced at War Cloud. The Coyotero narrowed his eyes.

Belcher sipped his coffee and stretched his upper lip back from his teeth as he swallowed. "Gentlemen, I submit to you that Black Twisted Pine brainwashed my dear Lucy into believing not only that he loved her, but that he could give her a better life than I can. He coerced her into believing that she should run away with him into the mountains of Mexico and live a pure, raw life out in the open air."

Leslie said, "How can you be so sure that she was brainwashed into believing this, Anson?"

"Because I found out from Kilroy . . . only *after* the incident," Belcher added disgustedly, "that Black Twisted Pine is a member of a secret religious sect inside the Chiricahua band of Apaches. A sect whose . . .

uh, mecca, if you will . . . is a mountain inside the
Shadow Montañas known as *Blood Mountain*."

Sitting to Longarm's left, War Cloud made a barely
audible sound. It was like a single organ chord emanating from deep in his chest. Magpie must have heard it,
too, because she turned her own questioning gaze to her
father.

"Heard of it?" Longarm asked his friend.

War Cloud said nothing.

Belcher said, "I'm told that the Chiricahuas don't
speak of it. A very secret thing. Quite private. Kilroy
heard about it from an old medicine man who, in his
later years, got a loose tongue . . . especially when he
overindulged in *tiswin*. The captain told me that Blood
Mountain is said to house the spirit of an Apache witch
who, during a special ceremony, bestows certain magi-
cal powers upon young women taken there. Powers that
turn them into sorceresses. *Witches*."

Leslie said, "Anson, you never told me this."

"What would be the point?" Belcher shrugged. "It's
all rot. A bunch of Apache hoodoo nonsense, though
having thought about it for a while now, I realize that
it's probably the same rot that Black Twisted Pine probably filled Lucy's head with."

"It's not nonsense to the Chiricahuas, Major," War
Cloud said tensely.

Belcher ignored him as though he weren't there. "It's
just the type of fanciful gibberish that would appeal to
her imagination and foolishly romantic sense of the
world. I'm sure this Blood Mountain is a place my wife
would find quite fascinating. A place where she thinks
she can confer with the spirit world and find the . . .

enlightenment . . . she's been looking for her entire life. And I've no doubt that that's where Black Twisted Pine has taken her . . . to commune with this Chiricahua witch. She no doubt believes she'll finally find the meaning of life, peace, and happiness there."

Face flushed with anger, Belcher sipped his coffee and brandy.

War Cloud turned to Longarm, said, "I've heard enough of this man's shit for one night, brother. I'll be heading back to the bunkhouse." He glanced at Magpie, who slid her chair back and rose, casting her cold stare at the major.

"Leaving so early?" Belcher said. "But the night is young, my Indian friends!"

War Cloud said, "You got no respect for the Apache way, Major. No respect for your wife. No respect for any woman. You don't even respect yourself, Major." The scout thrust an arm and an angry finger at his not so gracious host. "Men like you die hard deaths in Apache country!"

He barked something in his own Coyotero tongue to Magpie, and the two strode angrily toward the door leading to the foyer.

Belcher rose from his chair. "How dare you speak to me in that tone, you fucking heathen!"

War Cloud stopped and wheeled back to face the room. His eyes were wide and bright. He'd wrapped a hand around one of the Colts on his hips but managed to keep the weapon in its holster. His jaws were hard. Longarm could tell he was really talking with himself about not triggering a .44 round through Belcher's forehead.

Longarm had gained his feet, as had Leslie. He held his hands out, palms down, placatingly, and said in a soft, even tone: "Easy."

Belcher was glowering at War Cloud from beneath his knit brows, the soldier's face beet-red. War Cloud stared back at the man. Unlike most Apaches, he didn't mind meeting the gaze of a white man dead-on. He'd always been like that, Longarm knew. Even before he'd left the Apache world to mingle with the White Eyes. If this were anywhere except on a cavalry fort, and if he hadn't agreed to accept a job, Longarm knew that Major Belcher would be roughly one ounce heavier about now and as dead as a fence post.

War Cloud removed his hand from the walnut grips of his Colt, turned, and strode out into the foyer, Magpie close on his heels. The girl cast a quick glanced toward Longarm.

The front door clicked open and slammed closed. Longarm turned to Belcher, who had slid his angry gaze to the lawman.

He said, "If there were anyone else around who could track my wife and that savage of hers to their lair in the Shadow Montañas, I'd have him thrown in the guard-house awaiting court-martial."

Longarm said, "No, you wouldn't." He leveled a hard, threatening look at the man. "We're heading for those mountains first thing tomorrow, Major. We'll find your wife and Black Twisted Pine, and I'll do everything I can to bring your wife back here to Fort McHenry. Those are my orders. But no one except you said anything about bringing the woman's lover back, and I don't answer to you."

He walked to the door leading to the foyer and said without turning around, "Obliged for the meal, Major Belcher. I don't expect we'll be speaking again until me and War Cloud return."

In the foyer, he donned his hat and went out.

He crossed the boardwalk running along in front of the married officers' houses and stepped onto the parade ground. War Cloud and Magpie were walking away ahead of him. The sun was down but it was not yet dark.

Belcher's front door opened behind him. Longarm stopped and swung back around to see Leslie step out onto the porch of the major's house, drawing the door closed behind her.

"Longarm!"

Holding her skirts above her ankles, she hurried down the porch steps and ran to him, her rust-red hair bouncing on her shoulders, earrings flashing. She looked up at him with beseeching in her eyes green as amethysts. Those clear, lustrous orbs glinted in the fading salmon-gold light remaining in the clear sky vaulting over the fort.

"Please—I have to talk to you. In private."

"What about?"

She shook her head. "Later."

Leslie glanced around the parade ground. Uniformed men were walking here and there, silhouettes sliding around in the gloaming. The hum of separate conversations reached Longarm's ears.

A few of the men turned their heads toward him and Leslie and stopped talking, nudging others with elbows. They were obviously interested in what the major's

beautiful sister-in-law and the federal lawman were doing together.

Rumors spread like wildfires on remote military outposts.

"There's a wagon shed down by the stables, north side of the fort," she whispered. "I'm going to get changed, and I'll meet you there in a half hour." She turned to walk away before he could object.

Longarm stood outside with War Cloud while Sergeant Fitzpatrick lowered the flag to the melancholic strains of a young corporal bugling taps. War Cloud didn't seem to want to talk about Belcher, likely afraid of getting his neck up again, and that was fine with Longarm, who saw no need to get himself riled up again, either.

They had an assignment—one that was larger than both of them and Belcher, and one that concerned border security as much as preventing a flare-up of the Apache wars. They had to remember that Belcher wasn't the only one capable of sending American troops into Mexico. Lucille's father, the territorial governor, was even more of a threat.

Longarm and War Cloud had to do everything they could to get Mrs. Belcher if not back in the loving arms of her husband, at least safely back on the American side of the border.

War Cloud went to bed, grumbling. Longarm bit the end off a three-for-a-nickel cheroot and took a slow walk along the fort's perimeter, chewing up time, smoking, and thinking, as he made his nonchalant way to the fort's north side. An arroyo cut through a corner of the

fort, and there was plenty of greasewood and mesquites for modest cover.

Not that he didn't have the run of the fort, but to protect the girl's honor more than anything, he didn't want to be spied skulking around with Leslie McPherson.

He found the buggy shed just south of the arroyo, where the stock barns, hay barns, and corrals were sprawled across a broad pasture area along the twisting ravine. He came up to the shed—a long, low, pole-roofed building open on three sides—and sat on a covered rain barrel to await his coconspirator. He didn't know what Leslie wanted to speak to him about, but he thought a safe guess would be her sister.

When he'd been sitting on the barrel for a good twenty minutes, he checked the time by starlight on his Ingersoll. Fifteen minutes late. He'd begun to grow concerned when he heard the crunch of gravel in the arroyo thirty feet straight out in front of him.

Before he realized it, his instincts had caused his right hand to quickly slide the Colt .44 from the holster on his left hip. Just after he'd clicked the hammer back, the girl's voice rasped, "For God's sakes, don't shoot me, Longarm!"

The lawman depressed the Colt's hammer. "Sorry, Leslie. Old habit, I reckon."

He heard more gravel crunch and watched her indistinct shadow rise up out of the ravine. As he dropped down off the rain barrel and stepped deeper into the shadow of the barn, she came toward him, a Mexican-style shawl, or mantilla, wrapped over her head and shoulders. Beneath it she wore a black-and-white calico

blouse, a long, dark skirt, and black boots. She stopped two feet in front of him.

"Piece of work, isn't he?" she said, keeping her voice low.

"I'd bet my Colt against horse apples he don't have a whole lot of friends."

Leslie took one step closer. Her eyes beneath the lacy, black veil flashed in the starlight as did the ends of her front teeth revealed by her parted lips. "I love how you handled him. I've never seen anyone stand up to him like that before."

"Frankly, the man needs a bullet."

"I'd pay you to assassinate him but my father keeps a rather tight rein on my allowance, and I've never been adept at earning my own living."

Longarm chuckled at that. "What'd you want to see me about?"

"I got to thinking that, since I may never see you again, we should finish what we started earlier."

Chapter 14

Longarm gave a wry chuff. She had to be joking.

But as she stepped forward, wrapped her arms around his neck, rose up on the toes of her boots, and mashed her lips against his, he realized she wasn't.

He rolled his eyes around as she kissed him, kept her breasts planted firmly against his chest. She didn't seem to be wearing anything under her blouse—he could feel the outlines of her warm breasts flattened against him.

When he was sure they were alone out here—he'd only spied a couple of hostlers putting the horses to bed—he wrapped his arms around her. He lowered them, flattened his hands against her bottom. She didn't seem to be wearing anything down there, either.

As he worked her skirt up around her waist, she groaned and pressed more tightly against him. When he'd had enough of her skirt to make the maneuver possible, he placed his hands on her bottom again to feel only smooth, warm skin. Nope, no under frillies.

She really was serious.

"You realize this is probably against regulations," Longarm said, pulling his head away slightly. At the same time he ran his hand down the crack between her round, firm buttocks and touched the first two fingers of his right hand against her furred mound.

He gently parted the flesh.

"Oh," she cooed. "Oh . . . oh . . ." She drew a breath and arched her back, spreading her thighs slightly, and pressed her hips harder against his pelvis. "Too late now," she breathed.

They kissed some more while he probed her love nest with the tips of his fingers. His pants were growing painfully tight, so he said, "I think we can do better than this."

When he removed his fingers from her pussy, she gave a little shudder and heaved against him once more. He let her skirt drop and then took her by the hand and entered the shed. He looked around, the starlight revealing the outlines of a dozen or so wagons—mostly heavy-wheeled hay wagons and lumber drays.

But there was one black, red-wheeled buggy with what appeared leather seats and a tasseled canopy. Likely the major and the major's wife's buggy, for those rare occasions the Apaches allowed safe travel to Benson or Tombstone for dinner and a show at the local opera house.

"This here looks comfortable enough," Longarm said as with a grunt he leaned down and picked Leslie up in his arms.

He lifted her into the rear of the buggy. She flopped back, giggling delightedly, onto the rear, stuffed leather

seat. Longarm stepped up into the carriage and removed his cartridge belt.

When he had the gun and belt coiled on the seat beside her, Leslie playfully slapped his hands away and, leaning forward, began unbuttoning his pants while looking up at him, her smile flashing like quicksilver in the ambient light filtering through the shed's three open sides.

"I must say, Longarm, your cock has been a bone in my craw ever since I stroked it earlier. I couldn't have gone to sleep tonight, thinking about how wonderful such an impressive organ would feel between my legs."

She reached into his pants and balbriggans and withdrew the organ of topic. She cooed as she rubbed her cheek against the swollen head of Longarm's cock.

She whispered, "I take it you realize that both my sister and I have . . . um . . . rather strong desires. Out here at McHenry, it's been rather a dry go for me for a while. A girl can't waltz around a cavalry fort like a mare in season, you know, though some of these raw, young recruits have attracted my eye a time or two."

She licked the tip of his iron-hard shaft and glanced up at him again. "I've managed to be good . . . until now. When I saw you ride into the fort earlier, I just knew I had to have you."

"The visit to my room earlier wasn't totally innocent, you're sayin'?"

As she ran her tongue around the tip of his bulging mushroom head, she smiled devilishly and slowly shook her head.

Longarm laughed. It was cut off by a deep groan when she slid her mouth down farther on his cock.

After she'd sucked and lapped him for a while, he reached down, wrapped his hands around her arms, and lifted her to a standing position. He kissed her as he lowered his pants to his ankles. Sitting down on the seat, he lifted her onto his lap and twisted and pulled at her skirt until he had it up around her belly.

She was breathing hard now, staring down at him, her lips parted, eyes darkly erotic. He lifted her slightly and she reached between them, grabbed his cock and held it steady while he slowly lowered her bottom onto it.

He grunted and sighed as her warm insides, slick and wet, slid down, down until she was sitting flat across his hips, straddling him.

Her pussy contracted, grabbing at him, clutching him, causing sabers of sheer delight to fire through his belly and into his chest until his vision swam. He unbuttoned her blouse and slid both flaps back to expose her breasts. They bulged toward him, swollen with desire, nipples jutting. As she began rising up and down on her knees, he kneaded her breasts with his hands, rolling the nipples between his thumbs and index fingers.

"Oh," she said thickly as she continued to rise and fall. "Oh."

The buggy creaked slightly beneath them, the leather seat squawking faintly.

He could feel her warm fluid slither out around his shaft to lather his balls and the insides of his thighs.

Rolling her head back, causing her hair to slide around her shoulders and breasts, she made sounds that were somewhere between sobs of anguish and exclamations of excruciating delight.

"Oh, Longarm."

Longarm grunted, thrust his hips up, shoving his cock up hard inside her, moving in perfect concert with the girl's own maneuverings. He buried his face in her cleavage, ran his mustache and tongue up and down that deep, mysterious valley, and then lathered her nipples and sucked them, feeling them growing even harder.

She wrapped her arms around his head, pressed her lips to his forehead, pulled at his hair and his ears, raked her fingers across the back of his neck.

As more warm fluids oozed around his cock and her womb clutched at him harder, she groaned and mewled softly, consciously keeping a handle on her love screams so as not to bring running all the soldiers at the fort. Longarm's cock had a massive heart throbbing in it. It throbbed harder and harder, aching wonderfully.

He grunted and groaned and squeezed his eyes shut as he ground his heels against the buggy floor. His passion was rising quickly toward a crescendo. He leaned back against the seat.

Leslie gritted her teeth and lifted her chin, slowing her pace, grinding against him more deliberately, shivering as though deeply chilled, before lifting the lips of her love nest again to the head of his cock, then down over it again and twisting around on her knees. He thought his iron-hard piston was going to slam through some barrier within the girl and dislocate one of her ribs.

"Oh. Oh, God. Oh, God!" She wrapped her arms around his neck, thrust her pelvis hard against his, and leaned her head back so that her long hair tickled his thighs.

She convulsed violently, sucking back her love screams through her gritted teeth. Longarm grabbed her around the waist, bucked up hard against her, and felt a bomb explode within him. The blast blew up the dam he'd built against his passion, and his hot seed jetted into Leslie like the lava spewing from an angry volcano.

She groaned from deep in her chest and tossed her head from side to side, raking her silky hair across the tops of his thighs.

Longarm hung on to the girl hard and tipped his own head back as he continued to spend himself, gritting out, "Christ! *Christ!*"

Then he was finished but for one more sweet spasm.

Leslie lowered her head with a sigh, hair spilling down her cheeks, shoulders, and breasts. She leaned forward and pressed those beautiful, hot, sweat-slick orbs against his face, running her fingers through his hair.

"Oh, yes." She swallowed. He could feel her heart beginning to slow its hammering in her chest. She moved her shoulders, snuggling her breasts up tighter against his face. "Oh, yes—that will do nicely."

Longarm felt her swing her head toward the front of the shed. She gasped.

Longarm turned his head, as well. A silhouette turned in the shed's opening. It was the silhouette of a slender girl in a doeskin dress, with a broad belt wrapped around her waist. Starlight glittered on a sheathed knife and gun handle and in Magpie's long, stygian-black hair.

War Cloud's daughter disappeared around the corner of the shed, and Longarm heard the near-silent thuds of her moccasins growing fainter as she walked away.

Chapter 15

The arrow flew so close to Longarm's face that he felt the curl of warm against his nose before his ears registered the zing of the missile's passage. The dyed ash javelin thunked raucously against the stone outcropping rising on the left side of the trail.

Bang!

War Cloud lowered his smoking Spencer slightly. Longarm, his mind still whirling from his almost losing the end of his nose, jerked his gaze toward where his partner had fired.

A young Chiricahua Apache in traditional deerskins and red muslin bandanna stood between two boulders on the escarpment about thirty feet up from the trail. The short, dark brave grunted as he dropped his arrow, which clattered down the rocks of the slope, and then slumped forward, clapping both his dark hands to his belly. His knees bent. He pitched forward from the ledge he was on and turned one complete somersault before

landing in the trail about six feet in front of Longarm's and War Cloud's horses.

The mounts jerked with starts, nickering uneasily.

Longarm stared down at the brave who lay moaning, squeezing his eyes closed. The arrows that had tumbled out of his deerskin quiver when he'd fallen now crackled onto the rocks around him. They were fletched with the customary Chiricahua tribal designs. Blood pumped out of the hole in the brave's upper left chest.

Longarm reached forward and slid his Winchester from his saddle scabbard. He pumped a round into the breech one-handed, and held the rifle straight up on his right thigh.

Behind him and War Cloud, Magpie sat her buckskin tensely, pistol in her hand, looking around at the rocks lining this narrow corridor winding up into the higher reaches of the Shadow Montañas, the foothills of which they'd reached early the day before, two weeks after leaving Fort McHenry.

Until now, they'd seen no sign of the small band of wild Apaches who claimed these mountains as home.

"You see any more?" Longarm asked War Cloud, who was also casting his wary gaze around the escarpments looming on each side of the trail.

The scout shook his head.

Then he jerked his head around. Longarm saw the second Apache, then, too. The brave knelt between two boulders near where the first had fired from, drawing his nocked arrow back with a squawk of strained bear gut and ash wood.

Longarm snapped his rifle to his shoulder and fired at the same time the arrow went hurling toward War

Cloud, who'd neck-reined his horse around tightly, narrowly avoiding the missile.

"Down!" Longarm shouted as, racking another round into his Winchester's chamber, he leaped out of the saddle to hit the ground flat-flooted. He rammed his rifle against his horse's left hip. The dun whinnied and went screaming up the corridor with War Cloud's and Magpie's mounts. Squinting against the dust, Longarm shouted, "Haul ass into the rocks! I'll cover you!"

He dropped to a knee and aimed his Winchester up at the basalt and granite monoliths rising on the trail's south side, studded here and there with cedars. He saw a snake slither through a crack in the rocks and poke its head into a hole. It gave its button tail a little quiver before pulling it into the cliff face, out of sight with the rest of it.

In the periphery of his vision, Longarm saw War Cloud and Magpie run into the rocks and begin climbing the cliff, weaving amongst boulders and brush clumps. A half second later, three or four more Apaches appeared at nearly the same time, filling the gaps between rocks about thirty feet up the ridge.

They loosed arrows with tooth-gnashing twangs and ensuing whines. Longarm fired once, twice, three times and was aware of one Apache falling back out of sight while another tumbled onto the trail.

Longarm bolted off his heels and ran up a gravelly trough amongst the rocks and boulders hanging precariously suspended along the cliff face, arrows cracking off stone all around him from above. One smacked a thumb of rock to his right.

He stopped and jerked a look at an Apache standing

atop a finger of rock about twenty yards above and to
his left. As the Apache reached to pull another arrow
from his quiver, Longarm aimed and fired the
Winchester.

The warrior was thrown back with a yelp. The last
Longarm saw of him was his moccasins rising high in
the air before dropping back down the other side of his
perch.

Several shots rose on Longarm's left, in the direction
in which War Cloud and Magpie had run up the ridge.

The lawman racked a fresh cartridge and continued
running up the ridge, boots sliding in the loose shale.
He gained the top, breathing hard. Only one more shot
rose on his right, and then an eerie silence descended.

Longarm walked amongst the rocks topping the
ridge, looking slowly from his right to his left and back
again, tracking with his cocked rifle. The silence was
ominous. There was no movement except the breeze
occasionally lifting little swirls of dust.

Ahead, the gravelly slope dropped slightly. A corridor angled gradually off to Longarm's right.

Tufts of grass and twisted cedars grew amongst the
rocks that had obviously been spilled here during a long-
ago eruption of a massive volcano—one of many that
made up the Shadow Montañas, which were a maze of
black volcanic rock mixed with occasional basalt or
sandstone outcroppings.

Squeezing his Winchester in his hands, crouching,
Longarm walked slowly around the bend.

Just as the trail began to straighten, he caught movement in the periphery of his left eye. He jerked his head
and gun around in time to see a shirtless, middle-aged

Apache with long, black, silver-streaked hair aim a Colt's revolving rifle at him. The Apache squinted as he triggered the rifle, which must have been new to him— he'd probably swiped it from a prospector or some other white man he'd found interloping in these sacred mountains of the Chiricahuas—and missed Longarm by a foot.

The bullet plowed into rock ahead and above the lawman, spanging wickedly.

Longarm's Winchester roared twice. He watched the warrior jerk back against the rock wall behind him, snarling and triggering his rifle into the gravel near his knee moccasins. Blood pumped from the two holes in his leathery hide drawn taut across his ribs.

Something moved along the corridor ahead of Longarm. The lawman threw himself to his left a half second after an arrow broke against the rocks where he'd been standing a moment before.

He rolled off a shoulder and snapped the Winchester's rear stock to his cheek, taking quick aim at the Apache running toward him down the corridor, grimacing anxiously as he reached over his left shoulder to pluck another arrow from his quiver.

Longarm drew a bead on the Apache's chest over which a red-and-white calico blouse and medicine pouch billowed. The Apache howled wickedly, dark eyes flashing. When the brave was ten feet away from Longarm, the lawman squeezed the Winchester's trigger.

The hammer fell with a benign ping against the firing pin.

Longarm cursed.

The Apache stopped, grinned, and loosed his arrow. The missile was a blur hurling toward Longarm, who had no time to dodge before he felt the hot pain of the strap-metal head burying itself in his upper left arm.

Longarm yelped and dropped his empty rifle. He glanced at the arrow. About a foot of its back end protruded from the front of his left arm. The rest, including the blood-coated, strap-metal head, protruded from the back of that arm.

"Fuck!"

Should have counted your shots, dumbass . . .

Longarm rose to his knees and slid his Colt from its holster. But before he could get the weapon aimed, the Apache was on him.

The warrior kicked the gun out of the lawman's hand. The Colt barked, hurling its slug skyward before it went flying high in the air and careening back down the corridor in the direction from which Longarm had come.

The Apache took one step back and, crouching and grinning, slid a big bowie knife from a beaded sheath under a red slash on his right hip. He grinned wider, showing nearly a full set of large, crooked, yellow teeth, his long hair blowing in the breeze.

Longarm heaved himself quickly to his feet, stifling a yelp against the searing pain in his left arm, feeling the blood ooze out from both the entrance and exit wound. He spread his boots and squared his shoulders at the Apache, who crouched like a cat about to pounce. The Indian expertly flipped the knife in his hand and held it up slightly to show Longarm the razor edge.

Longarm's pulse hammered in his temples.

This didn't look good. This didn't look one bit good.

The Apache, short and muscular, with cunningly slanted eyes, appeared to be damn good with that knife . . .

There was nothing quite so fortifying as feeling as though you're teetering on a precipice with death yawning from the darkness below. As the Apache lunged toward Longarm, the lawman parried the blow with his left arm, screaming against the fire flaring in that arm when he knocked it against the Apache's knife hand.

The lawman lurched forward, hammering the Apache's left cheek with his right fist.

He'd found the strength to land a sledgehammer blow to the Indian's face. It scrambled the Native's brains for a valuable split-second, enough time for Longarm to deliver an on-target kick to the Chiricahua's crotch. He'd put enough adrenaline behind the kick that the Apache screamed and dropped the knife as he bent forward and clapped both forearms over his battered balls.

Instantly, the Indian straightened, tears glistening in his eyes from the pain he was trying to shrug off. He balled his fists and quartered around Longarm. The lawman reached around his left arm with his right hand, and screamed as he broke off the end of the arrow and tossed it away. He pulled the end out of the front of his arm with another bellowing yell that rocketed around the canyon.

He held the splintered end of the arrow in his right hand, blood dripping off the finger of split wood jutting from the main shaft.

"Here, you son of a bitch," Longarm raked out through clenched teeth, "maybe you'd like this back!"

The Indian had watched in hang-jawed amazement as the white man had removed both ends of the arrow

from his own arm. That's why he was slow to react when the same big man with the bloody left arm bolted toward him, hammering his left fist with another echoing scream across the Apache's right cheek.

The Apache grunted and stumbled backward.

The big lawman was on him in a second, grabbing him by the back of his neck and pulling his head forward while he rammed the splintered end of the bloody spear into the Apache's throat.

The brave stumbled back, screaming and clawing at the bloody shaft in his neck. He fell back against a wall of the canyon and, choking, frothy blood pumping from his neck, dropped to his butt before falling onto his shoulder and jerking as the last of his life bled out.

Two more figures appeared in Longarm's field of vision. He scooped the Apache's bowie knife off the ground and held the knife up in a ready crouch. But it was the War Cloud father and daughter standing there looking at him in mute amazement.

An Apache warrior was down on all fours in front of them—a tall, bony young man with an eagle feather headband. Obviously the War Clouds' prisoner, he too was staring skeptically up at the tall white man in the blue shirt and string tie, wielding the knife.

Longarm lowered the knife and straightened with a sigh.

"Where you two been?" he said. "And who's your friend?"

He'd barely gotten that last out before the ground started to pitch around him. Several clouds must have passed over the sun, because shadows skittered along the rocky canyon around him. He looked up. The sky

was clear. His brain was only just then catching up to his body, realizing the throbbing pain hammering him as blood continued to ooze out of both holes in his arm.

"You best sit down and rest, brother," War Cloud advised, glancing at Magpie with the unspoken order to watch their prisoner, and strode toward the lawman. "You don't look so good. Ouch—that arm's gotta hurt!"

Longarm glanced at the bloody appendage. "I gotta admit it's a might on the uncomfortable side." He looked around at the ridge walls. "We get all of 'em?"

"For now. There will likely be more. I don't know how large the band is that lives in these mountains—I haven't been here for many years, not since I was a wild young brave—but the Chiricahuas will try everything they can to keep trespassers away. Especially away from Blood Mountain, where they believe their witch god lives."

He peered toward the large, arrow-shaped formation that they'd been heading for in the southwest though the large, bald, black granite peak couldn't be seen from this vantage.

War Cloud took Longarm's good arm and led him over to the shaded side of the canyon. The scout shoved Longarm down onto his butt and pushed him back against the relatively cool stone wall. War Cloud looked at the two dead men, and then he looked at Longarm and shook his head.

"That was a piece of work there, brother." He chuckled and looked at Magpie, who offered a rare smile, her dark eyes flashing in the sunlight.

Longarm looked at the Apache brave whom Magpie was holding a pistol on. "Who's he?"

War Cloud looked at the Apache, whose left eye was swelling closed. Blood dribbled down from the young brave's left temple. "He will not tell me his name. Magpie knocked him out with a rock. He has been shamed. But do you see those two eagle feathers?"

"Someone important?"

War Cloud nodded. "Likely the son of the band leader—whoever he is. I figure if we have the leader's son with us, we will have an easier time reaching Black Twisted Pine."

"Good thinkin'."

Magpie said something to her father. War Cloud frowned at the girl and then, apparently to appease her, he walked back to stand over the young Apache, aiming his carbine at the brave's head.

Meanwhile, Magpie walked over and knelt down beside Longarm. She said something in her tongue that sounded like German being spat out around a mouthful of rocks, and lifted his wounded arm slightly. She lowered her head, squinting her eyes, evaluating both wounds.

Longarm glanced at War Cloud.

War Cloud frowned. The protective father was not pleased by the girl's ministrations. "He'll be all right," the scout groused at his daughter. "Hell, he's cut himself worse shaving."

"Thanks, brother," Longarm said with an ironic smile.

Magpie spat out a small stream of Coyotero at her father. It had an angry, chastising ring to it.

War Cloud flushed and glanced away, cowed.

Magpie lifted her head and shook back her hair as

she removed her loosely tied blue neckerchief. She spat some more Apache, telling Longarm something about stopping the bleeding until they could get to fresh water, and wrapped her neckerchief around his arm, covering both holes.

He watched her small, brown hands firmly but gently tie the neckerchief around his arm. He looked at her brown cheek behind the shifting curtain of her hair that she now let hang loosely about her shoulders, a style she'd started the day after she'd caught Longarm and Leslie McPherson fucking in the wagon shed at Fort McHenry.

The girl finished tying the neckerchief and glanced at the lawman. She caught him staring at her. She blinked, held his gaze, and then rose and walked away.

Longarm glanced at War Cloud. The scout gave him a dark look. Longarm gave a wry chuckle. He looked around cautiously. Judging by the long-angling shadows, he figured it was around four in the afternoon.

"We'd best get to the horses, ride for another hour or so, then find a place to camp."

"Sure you can ride, Custis?"

Longarm gained his feet. The pain was intense, but he'd suffered worse. He'd live. Once they found their horses he'd take a couple shots of rye or a belt of Major Belcher's brandy.

"I can ride," he said and strode off to fetch his rifle and revolver.

War Cloud gave the Chiricahua a savage kick to his backside and yelled in the brave's own tongue, "Dirty Chiricahua dog, get to your feet or I'll gut-shoot you and leave you here to the pumas!"

While Longarm and War Cloud were following their prisoner and the girl back toward where they'd left their horses, War Cloud sidled up to Longarm and said into his ear, "Remember what I said earlier?"

"About what?"

"About the curse my wife put on any white man who tries to make time with Magpie . . . ?"

"Oh, that one," Longarm growled. "How could I forget?"

War Cloud gave him an ominous grin.

Despite the warning, Longarm allowed himself a glance at the girl's perfectly shaped rump causing her doeskin dress to sway enticingly ahead of him.

Chapter 16

Horses were fearful but relatively stupid beasts, so their fear didn't often carry them far. That was why Longarm and the War Clouds had a mercifully short ways to walk in running them down. They also found the Apaches' horses and appropriated one for the brave.

The trio and their gagged and bound captive continued riding along the old Indian trail they'd been following since entering the range. All three allies scoured the terrain around them every step of the way.

They rode higher and higher into the Shadow Montañas, and after cresting one of several ridges stippled with the flora of the high desert, the peak they were heading for rose into spectacular view straight ahead of them, vaulting back against the southeastern sky. And with the sun angling down in the west, behind the riders, the flame-shaped monolith showed why the name of Blood Mountain had been hung on it. Late in the day the setting sun made the chunk of ancient black granite

and hardened volcanic lava fairly glow the crimson of fresh blood.

It was quite a sight jutting there beyond several more rocky, pine-carpeted ridges, and though Longarm guessed they were still a good day's away from it, the lens-clear light cast in vibrant relief its scalelike pocks, fissures, thumbs, cornices—all tapering to a peak resembling a giant, deftly crafted arrowhead.

When the sun was nearly down, Longarm reined up beside the trail, at the edge of fragrant pines growing amongst the rubble of spewed lava boulders, and reached back with his right hand to fish his field glasses out of his saddlebags. He grumbled against the pain in his wounded arm, cursing himself again for not having counted his shots, and held the field glasses up to his face.

"They are still there, brother," War Cloud said. "Seen 'em from atop the last ridge."

Longarm cursed.

For the past three days, he and War Cloud had been aware of two shadowers. At least, he thought there were two. They'd remained far enough behind Longarm's party that the lawman had never gotten a clear view of them. Thus, he had no idea who they were. They could have been banditos they'd picked up after they'd crossed the border into Mexico, or they could have been a couple of riders whom Major Belcher had sent to follow Longarm and the War Clouds out from Fort McHenry.

The lawman thought the latter possibility the most likely. Banditos would either have accosted their quarry by now or lost interest and disappeared from their trail.

"I think we'd best find out who they were before we

get any closer to Blood Mountain and Black Twisted Pine," Longarm said, returning the glasses to their case. "Let's hole up here, go without a fire. Maybe they'll ride up on us."

They looked around for a place to camp. Magpie found a spring running out from the base of a stony dike and dribbling off into a freshet curling amongst the pines. Being high and well sheltered by boulders and tall trees, it was a good place to camp.

They tended their horses and the brave's pinto mustang first and then arranged their gear in a sandy area at the base of the dike, the freshet running down the slope nearby. War Cloud tied the prisoner securely with rope to a tree, and the young brave sat, coldly staring.

Longarm sat on a rock ledge jutting from the dike. He set his saddlebags and canteen down beside him and took a long drink of water, cutting through the dryness in his throat.

When he'd corked the canteen and fished a bottle out of his saddlebags, needing another couple of shots to dull the pain in his arm, Magpie walked over and grabbed the bottle out of his hand.

"Hey!" Longarm said.

She spat some Chiricahua at him, and then set the bottle on a rock by his saddlebags and began untying the bandage around his arm.

"She says to make sure there is enough for cleaning the wound," War Cloud said. He was sitting cross-legged on the far side of their little, bowl-shaped camp, taking apart his rifle and cleaning each part with an oily rag. "She acts like she's your mother or something."

He chewed out several sentences to his daughter in

their language. Magpie ignored him. She unbuttoned Longarm's shirtsleeve and then sat with his hand in her lap, gently cleaning his arm with the whiskey.

Longarm sat gritting his teeth at the infernal sting in each of the holes in his arm. If she was aware of the pain she was causing him, the girl didn't let on. She continued to very slowly, methodically, and gently clean the dried and jellied blood away from each hole—it was a clean flesh wound—with the bandage soaked in whiskey.

When she had his arm clean, she scurried off up a near slope and came back with a handful of what appeared plant root and pine needles. War Cloud sat watching his daughter in mute frustration as he continued to thoroughly clean his rifle. Magpie placed the root powder and pine needles in a fresh, whiskey-soaked bandage, and wrapped the bandage tightly around the lawman's wounded arm.

When she was finished, she spoke to him in Chiricahua, and War Cloud translated:

"You are to keep the arm as still as possible tonight, to let the medicine do its work, keep the wounds from festering. By tomorrow, you will be good as new. But if you think this means we're getting married or anything, you're badly mistaken, White Eyes. You make a play for me, that donkey cock of yours will swell up, turn as black as an old dog turd, and fall off!"

War Cloud snickered devilishly as he reassembled his rifle. Magpie turned to her father, scowling.

Longarm snorted and popped the cork on his bottle of Tom Moore. There was still a goodly portion of the

elixir left. He took several pulls and was glad to feel some relief in the burning of his arm.

An owl hooted in the far distance. It was a forlorn-sounding cry in the dusky silence. Longarm stared tensely in the direction from which it had come. War Cloud gazed in the same direction, sliding the loading tube out of the rear stock of his Spencer repeater and hastily filling it with fresh .56-caliber rounds from his shell belt.

It might have really been an owl. But Longarm didn't think so. Obviously, War Cloud didn't, either. And neither did their Chiricahua captive.

The brave sat back against the pine to which he was tied, slanting his eyes in a menacing, knowing smile.

"None of us best sleep too deep tonight, brother," War Cloud advised.

"Hell," Longarm said, feeling the short hairs rise across the back of his neck, "I never sleep a wink in 'Pache country."

Longarm took the second watch while War Cloud and Magpie relaxed, maybe dozing occasionally, in their fireless hollow amongst the rocks and pines.

The lawman's arm ached. He didn't want to get drunk and nod off, but he kept his traveling flask in the pocket of his frock coat, taking a modest, medicinal sip every now and then.

He walked slowly around the camp, navigating by the light of a sickle moon and the stars that were clear and sharp at this high elevation. It was cool here, too, and his breath plumed thinly as he breathed.

Despite the brandy, his senses were knife-edged. That was due to the raking fear any white man felt in Apache country. If he and the War Clouds were captured alive, they'd likely pray to die. No one could inflict more grisly horror on a man's . . . and a young woman's . . . body than an Apache. Especially when their victims had been trespassing on said Apaches' sacred ground.

That was a transgression that piss-burned Apaches like no other. Fortunately, it was said there weren't many Chiricahuas remaining in the Shadow Montañas, that the sect that followed the witch-god religion, or whatever the Apaches called it, had all but died off.

Of course, Longarm and the War Clouds had no right to be here. But they'd been assigned to this secret mission to bring Mrs. Belcher back to her husband and forestall a possible flare-up of the war with the Chiricahuas—not mention avoid a dustup with Mexico—so they had good reason to be here. Or good enough for Longarm. He had a job to do, and he was going to do it.

What he'd do if Mrs. Belcher didn't want to return to her husband, he had no idea. There was no point in thinking about that yet. Best to walk the trail one step at a time . . .

Longarm stood between two tall pines, staring toward the large, black silhouette of Blood Mountain glistening in the moonlight like polished obsidian. He twisted around and sat down quickly, doffing his hat to make himself a smaller shadow. He held the Winchester low so that the light wouldn't reflect off the barrel.

Beneath the quiet rasp of his own breathing, he'd

heard something. It came again. The thud of a hoof. Followed by another.

The sounds faded and then rose again and became more regular. Apaches?

As if in answer to the lawman's question there was the ring of iron on stone. That meant at least one of the horses was shod. Apaches didn't shoe their horses. The riders coming along the same trail that Longarm and the War Clouds had been traveling were either gringos or Mexicans. Most likely, they were the same two who had been following Longarm's party for the past few days.

The lawman's heart increased its beat.

Slowly, he rose and made his way very slowly and quietly down the slope toward the trail. The thuds of the slowly approaching riders continued to grow.

When he reached the trail, he hunkered down between a piñon and a boulder. He doffed his hat again and edged a look around the boulder and along the trail meandering through the brush and rocks, rising and falling gently—a chalky pale thread in the darkness.

Two jostling shadows moved toward him. They were riding single file. The first rider was small and dark. The one he glimpsed behind the first appeared fair. Starlight twinkled off bridle chains and bits. Now he could hear their horses breathing and the squawk of saddle leather.

When they were twenty yards away from him, Longarm stepped out into the trail, glowering. He'd seen the long, red hair on the second rider.

Keeping his voice low but pitched with fury, he said,

"What in God's name do you two think you're doing out here?"

Both horses jerked with starts. The first one on which rode Major Belcher's housekeeper, Blue Feather, turned sideways, shaking its head. The second horse came on at a frightened trot and stopped slightly ahead of the first horse when Leslie McPherson sawed back on the reins.

"Christ!" she rasped, more startled than her horse. "Longarm, is that *you* . . . I hope . . . ?"

Blue Feather had reached into the scabbard strapped to her saddle and withdrew a Winchester carbine. She held it across her saddlebows, her wide, dark eyes sharply reflecting the starlight.

"You're damn lucky it's me!"

Longarm strode up between the two women and their blowing horses, shifting his angry gaze from one to the other. Leslie wore black denims and a denim jacket over a pearl blouse, a tan slouch hat on her head. Blue Feather wore buckskin breeches and a calico blouse with a blue bandanna on her head, knotted behind.

"I had to come, Longarm," Leslie said. "I knew I was taking a hell of a chance, but when Blue Feather told me she knew this country, I . . ."

"Two women riding alone in Apache country is insane. You're damn lucky you're still alive. We ran into a pack of 'em only a few hours ago."

Leslie looked at his arm. "Are you hurt?"

"Not bad but my point is you could be in their camp about now, and they could . . ." He saw no reason to continue the thought. "Ah, Christ. Get off those mounts and we'll lead 'em back to our camp. Now that you're

here, you're here, and we have to figure out what to do with you."

The women dismounted and followed Longarm off the trail and up the rise through the boulders and pines.

As they approached the camp, Longarm quietly hailed War Cloud, whom he found standing with his rifle aimed atop a boulder snag. The scout had no doubt heard the riders before they'd even reached Longarm. Magpie was crouched behind a ponderosa, but now she stepped out and tilted her head to one side, peering incredulously at their unexpected guests.

War Cloud whistled and depressed his Spencer's heavy hammer. "Whoo-ee," the scout said softly. "That sure wasn't a good idea, Miss Leslie." He spoke to Blue Feather in her own tongue. The young Apache woman kept her features as expressionless, ignoring him.

Longarm fumed as he led the women to where his and the War Clouds' horses were tied in the heavy brush. As if he didn't have enough trouble—now he had two more women to worry about!

Chapter 17

"What in the hell were you thinking?" Longarm asked Leslie when the women's horses had been tended and tied with the others.

The party that had grown to five sat forming a ragged circle in the bowl of sandy ground in which they'd spread their gear, near the captive whom War Cloud had gagged in order to keep the brave from calling out to any of his brethren who might be lurking around.

Leslie leaned back against a rock, beside Blue Feather, knees raised, her arms around them. "I had to come and talk personally to my sister. You don't know her, Custis. No one understands her better than I do. Only I know how hard her marriage has been on Lucy. I don't think she'll come back if she knows she has to return to Anson Belcher. And I don't blame her. The only way she'll come back is if I can convince her she won't have to return to him, that I will help her get away

from that man. You see, she's almost as afraid of our
father as she is of Anson. I want to convince her that
we'll form a united front against both men."

Longarm considered what she'd told him. "Still," he
said, "this was a damn stupid ploy, Leslie. War Cloud
and I were sent to slip across the border—just two men
because two were less likely to be discovered than a
whole pack."

Leslie looked at Magpie. "What about her?"

"She's War Cloud's daughter and she can carry her
own weight. Hell, she can track as well as either one of
us can."

He glanced at the young Coyotero woman. Magpie
was favoring Leslie with a hard stare. That look almost
convinced Longarm that she was as much a threat to
Leslie as any of the Chiricahuas.

Leslie ignored the girl and turned to Longarm. "Well,
we're here now—Blue Feather and I. And we're staying
with you. And I think you'll see that I'm much more of
an asset and less of a liability than you think. Especially
when you meet my sister."

She glanced at War Cloud. "How much farther do
we have before we reach Black Twisted Pine's camp?"

War Cloud sat near their prisoner, one knee raised,
an arm resting on it. "Less than a day now if he is where
I think he will be—at the base of Blood Mountain. And
if he is in the Shadow Montañas, that is most likely
where we will find him."

"The mountain gives strength to women?" Leslie
asked.

"That is what Black Twisted Pine's people believe.
Chiricahua women who've become sick in their souls go

there to have their souls restored by the witch god who lives in the mountain. She in fact gives strength to all Chiricahuas who go there and perform the sacred rites—but women she endows with a special strength. Many come away from there not only healed, but they themselves become healers."

Leslie nodded thoughtfully. "I can see why Lucy wanted to be taken there. Black Twisted Pine must love her very much to have done this for her."

"Well, I just hope she'll be ready to leave when we finally catch up to her," Longarm said.

War Cloud added, "I just hope the Chiricahuas won't be too angry that we have trespassed on their sacred territory . . . and killed several of their own warriors in getting here."

Longarm winced. "There's that, too." He glanced at their young prisoner with the two eagle feathers in his hair. "At least we have him. Won't hurt to give the Chiricahuas some incentive not to shoot first and ask questions later."

"Your arm," Leslie said, rising and walking over to him. "Let me have a look—"

Magpie leaped to her feet and rushed over, growling in Apache and pointing at where Leslie had been sitting. Leslie looked flabbergasted.

"My gosh," she said, clapping a hand to her chest and glancing at War Cloud. "What's she saying?"

War Cloud chuckled and shook his head. "She says to leave her medicine alone and set your . . . um . . . to go sit down and leave the big man alone. She will tend him."

"Well, excuse me," Leslie said, glaring at Magpie, who glared back at her.

"Ladies, please," Longarm said.

War Cloud sighed and grabbed his rifle. "I'm going to keep watch."

"You've had your turn," Longarm said, reaching for his Winchester. "It's still my watch."

"Ah, hell, Custis—I won't be able to sleep a wink with all these women around. You stay here. I doubt either one of those two is going to let you out of their sight, anyway."

With that, the scout strode off, his rifle on his shoulder.

Longarm looked at the women still staring at each other and then grabbed his rifle. He needed to get away from the woman-heavy camp as much as War Cloud did.

He said, "You all stay here. Don't go wandering off."

"Where are you going, Custis?" Leslie asked.

"Off to look for a little peace and quiet," he grumbled as he climbed a low ridge north of the camp.

Longarm didn't realize he'd fallen asleep leaning back against a boulder until someone nudged him awake. He gave a startled grunt and started to raise the Winchester he'd been holding across his thighs, when he saw War Cloud squatting beside him.

"Easy, amigo," the scout said, glancing at the sky. "First light."

Longarm looked around. Sure enough, a couple of hours had passed. The first faint pearl light of the false dawn was lightly brushed across the sky in the east. The monolith of Blood Mountain stood in black relief against it.

He moved his wounded arm, winced against the heavy, dull pain of the arrow wound. As War Cloud started down the slope toward the camp, where all three women were sleeping curled in their blankets, and their captive brave sat back against the pine he was tied to, Longarm plucked his flask from his inside coat pocket and took a good-sized pull.

That eased the pain somewhat. He returned the flask to its pocket and then stiffly gained his feet and followed the scout down to the camp obscured by misty gray shadows.

Quietly, they grabbed their gear and hauled it off to where the horses were tied about forty yards away, at the base of the northern ridge. They glanced at each other conspiratorially over the backs of their horses, having decided what they were going to do without discussion.

Longarm rigged up his own horse and the brave's. When he had filled his two canteens at the freshet and hung the strap over his saddle horn, he saw the three young women moving toward him and War Cloud, weaving through the trees.

"Why didn't you wake us?" Leslie said, blinking sleep from her eyes.

"Because you're not going."

Leslie stopped. So did Blue Feather, still so groggy that she almost ran into Leslie. Magpie kept coming, stooped beneath the weight of the saddle she carried on her shoulder.

Leslie said, "What're you talking about? I came all this way to see my sister, and that's exactly what . . ."

She let her voice trail off, frowning angrily as

Longarm shook his head. He slid his Winchester into its saddle boot and walked over to the girl. At the same time, War Cloud spoke firmly in Coyotero to his daughter, gesturing vehemently with his hands.

Longarm looked down at Leslie frowning up at him. "You and Blue Feather are staying here. Magpie's going to stay with you, make sure you don't come after us."

"No, Custis! I'm—"

Longarm pressed two fingers to the girl's rich lips, cutting her off. He tried a tender, sympathetic smile. "I know you're concerned about your sister. But War Cloud and I will have an easier time getting into Black Twisted Pine's camp if it's just him and me and our prisoner. I promise I'll tell Lucy you're here and that you want to see her. That'll likely give her added incentive to leave. If all goes according to plan, she'll be with us when we return later this afternoon."

Leslie opened her mouth to protest, but closed it again when she saw the stern, stubborn look on Longarm's face.

"You follow us again," he told her in a deep, commanding voice, "I'll spank your bare ass and tie you to the nearest tree."

Leslie's eyes widened. She flushed, glanced at War Cloud, who had his lips compressed, holding back a snicker.

Magpie didn't look happy, either. She obviously wanted to finish the journey she'd started, but it appeared that she was going to abide by her father's wishes and remain here with Leslie and Blue Feather. Magpie would act as both prison guard and protector in the event that any Chiricahuas happened upon the camp.

It was a scowling trio of young women whom Longarm and War Cloud rode away from ten minutes later, Longarm leading the mustang of their captive young Chiricahua, who remained gagged and tied to his mount. When the party reached the trail, they headed north toward Blood Mountain shouldering ominously back against the lightening eastern sky.

Soon, if they were lucky, they'd find Lucy Belcher and her lover, Black Twisted Pine. If they were even luckier—probably a lot luckier—they'd be alive to see another sunset.

Given the Chiricahuas' particularly excruciating torture methods, Longarm just hoped that he and War Cloud would want to be.

Chapter 18

As they rode through the early morning, following the Indian trail through low hills carpeted in forest and then around the shoulders of eroded bluffs and tabletop mesas, forever rising and falling over the harsh terrain, Blood Mountain seemed to remain an unwavering distance away from them.

It was almost as though the mountain were sliding ever backward away from Longarm, War Cloud, and their captive just as they tried futilely to reach it. Longarm didn't have trouble imagining that there was indeed a female spirit inside the mountain—one that enjoyed laughing at foolish men trying to court her.

War Cloud took the lead, following the trail, his rifle resting on his right shoulder. Their gagged brave with the eagle feather headband rode behind, his mustang's reins tied to the tail of War Cloud's mount. Longarm rode behind the lad, keeping his Winchester aimed at the middle of the kid's slender back.

War Cloud stopped suddenly. He peered to his right, pointed out a thin puff of dark smoke unfurling skyward. Just as the cloud thinned, another rose to replace it, and then another and another, irregularly spaced. War Cloud didn't need to explain the significance of the smoke to Longarm. The lawman knew they'd been spied, and the smoke was most likely meant to warn the main camp of interlopers.

So far, however, they'd seen no Chiricahuas themselves. In fact, the only movement they'd seen at all in these godforsaken hills were coyotes, a rattlesnake trailing a jackrabbit, and one golden eagle hunting the crest of rocky dike.

War Cloud glanced over his shoulder at Longarm, who met his partner's cautious gaze. Then the scout touched moccasin heels to his horse's flanks, and continued forward, jerking the brave's mustang along behind him. Longarm followed, staying close to the brave, keeping his index finger curled through his Winchester's trigger guard.

Roughly fifteen minutes later, there was a soft, ominous whistle followed by a thud. Again, War Cloud stopped his horse abruptly, as did Longarm. Both men stared down at the arrow angling into the red clay dirt to the right of the trail.

They were between two sandstone outcroppings. A bare-chest Chiricahua in deerskin breeches stood atop the outcropping on the right. Another stood atop the one on the left. The one on the left aimed a rifle at War Cloud and Longarm.

The brave on the right outcropping stepped forward and dropped ten feet straight down the pile of eroded,

tan rock to land flat-footed and bent-kneed on a flat
boulder only a few feet from where the arrow protruded
from the ground. The remaining brave atop the left pile
of rock steadied his rifle threateningly.

The brave on the boulder near the trail scowled at
War Cloud and Longarm, then his molasses-dark eyes,
ringed with ochre dye, shifted to the interlopers' captive. He spoke angrily in his native tongue too quickly
for Longarm to follow.

War Cloud spoke to the stocky Chiricahua in his own
tongue, using sign language that included liberal gesturing with his arms and hands. He finished with a dark
glance back at his and Longarm's hostage and made an
angry slashing motion across his throat.

The brave on the boulder glared at War Cloud. Then
he glanced up at the brave standing atop the left escarpment. He threw his right hand up angrily and barked
briefly at War Cloud.

The scout glanced back at Longarm, jerked his chin
to indicate they would continue, and then touched heels
to his horse's flanks once more, starting forward.

Longarm put his own horse forward, glancing at the
brave on his right and then at the one on his left. His
wounded arm ached more than ever as his pulse
throbbed in his temples, and his throat went dry. The
last way he wanted to leave this world was by being
slow-roasted in a large clay pot over a Chiricahua
campfire . . .

When he and War Cloud had ridden about two hundred more feet, he glanced back. The Chiricahuas were
gone. In the south, the smoke signals were beginning
to rise again.

He felt a bead of cold sweat dribble down between his shoulder blades when he saw several figures clad in white and red run up the side of a distant hogback, weaving amongst trees and boulders. Longarm and War Cloud must have been approaching the Chiricahua camp, and the men ahead of him were pickets signaled by whoever was sending up the smoke.

Behind Longarm, hooves thudded. He looked back again to see the two braves they'd just passed now following from about two hundred feet behind, straddling white-and-brown paint mustangs with blanket saddles and braided horsehair hackamores.

Longarm followed War Cloud and their captive up the hogback the Apache pickets had been on and checked their mounts down at the crest. Blood Mountain suddenly appeared so close in the clear, dry air that Longarm almost believed he could reach out and run his hand across its scaly surface that was not blood colored at this time of the day but a darker shade of tan.

But its nearness was a mirage.

Below him, down the far side of the hogback, a deep, airy bowl opened, revealing the small, light-brown clumps of brush houses that Longarm knew to be wickiups—traditional Apache dwellings that fit the Natives' nomadic lifestyle in that they were easy to take down and put up again. The hovels were thumb-sized from Longarm's vantage.

The canyon—walled off on the far side by Blood Mountain itself—must have been a good five hundred yards across. A single cook fire burned. At the moment it was not being tended. A dozen or so men of various

ages walked out away from the small makeshift village to stare up at Longarm's party.

The warriors were either wielding bows and arrows or rifles—in some cases, both.

War Cloud glanced at Longarm and then started down the slope toward the waiting warriors. Longarm said fatefully under his breath, "Here we go," and put his own horse down the ridge, following a switchbacking trail. He kept his rifle aimed at the back of their hostage, hoping that consideration for the brave's life would keep any of the warriors from squeezing off a bullet or an arrow at either himself or War Cloud.

On the ridge above and behind him, one of the two braves who'd been following yelled down at the others. The warriors in the canyon glanced around at one another. A low hum of Chiricahua chatter rose briefly, and then all eyes returned to the visitors.

Longarm kept his finger taut against his rifle's trigger as he followed the other two horses down the steep slope. Lower and lower they rode, dropping down toward the canyon at the base of Blood Mountain.

When they reached the canyon floor, Longarm followed War Cloud and the tied and gagged brave ahead toward the waiting group of hard-eyed warriors flanked by the wickiups, the smoking fire, and the mountain wall beyond.

It was a small band, Longarm saw. About thirteen men of various ages, none appearing much over forty. They were a young renegade band who'd remained defiantly in the Shadow Montañas, likely to keep their sacred ground unspoiled by whites until, ideally, the

Apache nation had run all the whites entirely out of their
territory.

As he approached the group, Longarm saw that he
had been wrong about there being no one older than
forty here. Lingering beyond the others was a stocky
oldster with coal-black hair but a face much more wiz-
ened and craggy than the others.

Clad in doeskin the color of lamb's wool and adorned
with colored beads and porcupine quills, he sat on rock
near the fire. He was a small man with a pinched-up
face and deep-set eyes. He held a long, ceremonial spear
trimmed with colored feathers in his right hand, straight
up and down on the ground.

This man, an old chief and leader of the Blood Mountain protectors, remained sitting on his rock and staring
through eyes that were hard to see back within their
deep, sun-seared sockets.

One of the warriors—a tall, broad-shouldered hombre wearing a deerskin tunic, his hair in braids—
stepped forward. He, too, had painted rings around his
eyes and three periwinkle blue slashes on each cheek.
He walked up in front of War Cloud's horse and by the
way the two men looked at each other, Longarm knew
that they'd found Black Twisted Pine.

The two men said nothing for what seemed an hour
but was probably only a minute or so.

"So they sent you," Black Twisted Pine said finally,
gravely, wrinkling one of his broad nostrils. He was a
handsome man despite fairly close-set eyes and a high
forehead. Longarm thought he was probably as tall as
he himself was. A proud, straight, broad-shouldered
Chiricahua with a regal bearing.

"Not to kill," War Cloud said, holding up his right hand, palm out. "We want only the girl, my friend."

Black Twisted Pine seemed to flinch at that. The others around him didn't appear to understand English. They kept their angry gazes on Longarm and War Cloud, saying nothing.

Black Twisted Pine said, "You came here . . ."

"To take Mrs. Belcher back to the fort, my friend. It is the best way for your people and the White Eyes. The major is very angry. His father, the governor, is very angry. The governor has made the Great White Father in Washington very angry, as well. No good can come of this."

Black Twisted Pine looked at their bound and gagged captive. "You have dishonored our chief, Stalking Puma"—he glanced over his shoulder at the old man sitting on his rock—"by trussing up his grandson as though he were a calf for the white man's branding irons."

"We will let him go, my friend, if you give us your word we will not be harmed. We have done this to the brave only for our own protection. We did not mean to dishonor the chief. We came here only to speak to Mrs. Belcher in hopes that we can convince her to return to Fort McHenry with us."

Black Twisted Pine stared obliquely up at his ex-partner and then switched his gaze to Longarm. Repressed emotion caused his brows to wrinkle slightly. And then he said, "You want to see Mrs. Belcher? Put your weapons down and come—I will take you to her."

Longarm and War Cloud shared a look. Then Longarm depressed his Winchester's hammer and slid the

long gun into its scabbard. As War Cloud sheathed his own rifle, Black Twisted Pine spoke to the Chiricahuas flanking him. Several lurched forward, drawing knives from belt sheaths. Longarm froze for an instant, staring at the blades winking in the afternoon sun, but then the three braves surrounded his captive's horse and began sawing at the ropes tying him to his saddle.

War Cloud strode south, past the old man still sitting his rock, his wrinkled face implacable, and along the camp's perimeter. War Cloud and Longarm followed, both men looking around tensely at the other Chiricahuas. None appeared to be about to toss a knife or loose an arrow at them. That eased the worms of tension wringling up and down Longarm's spine only a little.

He was on foot now without his horse or his Winchester, and he and War Cloud were outnumbered. He could still end up in a large clay pot hung over the cook fire now smoking to his left as he and War Cloud followed Black Twisted Pine to the far southern end of the camp.

Blood Mountain rose nearly straight up at the far eastern end of the camp, the west-angling sunlight glistening on its stony surface, taking away all relief so that it looked like a massive, polished marble slab. Now it was a shiny brown. When the sun angled lower in the west, it would turn the color of blood.

Longarm and War Cloud followed Black Twisted Pine down a gradual slope. Ahead, a weird noise grew gradually louder. A warbling sound. The ridge on the right rose more steeply, narrowing the canyon between that ridge and the wall of Blood Mountain. Both Longarm and War Cloud stopped abruptly. They stared into the canyon that was roughly seventy yards across.

Longarm felt a tingling in his gut.

Ahead were a dozen or more crude scaffolds of peeled pine logs and branches. Now Longarm realized what was making the warbling sound. Birds of several varieties, including magpies and crows—all carrion-eaters—were milling around the scaffolds. They were also scrounging the bones littering the canyon floor. Skulls, thigh bones, rib cages, hands, feet . . .

All human.

"Christ," Longarm heard himself mutter.

War Cloud stood beside him, staring gravely toward Black Twisted Pine who strode through the strewn bones, between the scaffolds. The bird's squawking and barking grew louder, angrier. Several birds took flight while others defiantly held their ground. War Cloud's scout's deep chest rose and fell heavily as his severe gaze studied the bones and scaffolds.

A Chiricahua burial ground.

Black Twisted Pine stopped suddenly and turned back toward Longarm and War Cloud. He beckoned angrily. "Come!" he yelled. "You wanted to see Mrs. Belcher. I am taking you to her!"

Chapter 19

"She is with Ta-Ki-O-May—Woman God who resides inside the mountain and gives strength to all who come to her. To women, she gives a special strength. I wish to believe that Ta-Ki-O-May gave that special strength to Lucy, who needed it most of all, before she died, and that she has it now inside the Mountain Spirit. I wish there were other women here, to console her, but there is only Stalking Puma's braves—here to protect this sacred ground until it is safe for our entire band, the Blood Mountain People, to come and live here again."

Black Twisted Pine stared up into the scaffold that had been erected beyond all the other ones. It was the newest scaffold, its poles unskinned, and it stood at a point where the canyon began to dogleg to the west. Longarm followed Black Twisted Pine's gaze at the hide-wrapped body resting on the woven bed of brush extended between the scaffold's four legs. The body was entirely wrapped though the birds had worked loose a

bit of the deerskin at the top, and some locks of red hair protruded to blow around in the wind.

Three large crows were on the body, pecking at it. Black Twisted Pine did nothing to interfere. It was the natural order. Lucy Belcher was dead and her body would feed the living until her bones were strewn down on the canyon floor with the others. Then, in time, her bones would be dust.

The body did not matter to the Chiricahua. Only the spirit mattered.

Longarm was still trying to work his mind around what he'd been told. *Lucy Belcher was dead.*

"How?" he asked Black Twisted Pine.

"Belcher."

Longarm stared at the man, who continued to stare up at the scaffold until he turned to Longarm, his eyes hard and angry. "I went to the Belcher house early in the morning like I always did, to split firewood and help Mrs. Belcher start the day. I sensed something was wrong, so I went upstairs. Their bedroom door was open. I went in and found Belcher passed out, holding a bloody knife to his chest. Lucy lay beside him, dead. Stabbed. Belcher woke up. He was covered in blood and he smelled like whiskey. He was confused, but when he realized what he'd done he blamed me. He told me that Lucy had told him that she and I were going to go away together. So he killed her in a drunken rage and passed out. He laughed and told me to go ahead and take her . . . to take Lucy if I loved her so much . . . and he hoped we would have a very beautiful life together!

"I was in shock, but I wanted to kill him. Only, he had a gun on me. He didn't use it because he didn't want

to alert anyone else around the fort. I took Lucy. I had told her about Blood Mountain, and she wanted very badly to come here and live and to be given the strength she'd wanted for so long. In my sorrow, I thought that perhaps the goddess in the mountain would bring Lucy back to me. So I took Lucy, saddled two horses, and rode out away from the fort under cover of darkness."

He stopped and looked down. Tears dribbled down Black Twisted Pine's rugged cheeks.

Longarm glanced at the scaffold once more, grinding his molars on the fury he felt for Belcher. The major had killed his wife in a fit of jealous rage and then told her father that she'd run off with Black Twisted Pine. Was the man so deep in his proverbial and literal cups that he didn't think that Longarm and War Cloud would learn the truth?

Black Twisted Pine said tightly, "I vowed that one day I would go back across the border and I would kill Major Belcher. Until then, I would remain here and protect this sacred ground with my brothers."

A voice rose from the rocky western slope: "I'm sorry you won't have that opportunity, renegade!"

Longarm jerked his head toward the slope, and felt his lower jaw loosen when he saw the blue-clad soldiers standing there amongst the rocks. Belcher was at the center of the group. He was flanked by Captain Kilroy, who didn't look any too happy about being there. There were five other soldiers—three privates, Sergeant Fitzpatrick, and a corporal.

"How in the hell . . . ?" Longarm said, aghast.

"We just followed my sister-in-law and my housekeeper," Belcher said through a self-satisfied grin. "You

were probably so busy keeping an eye on them that you didn't look far enough back to see us."

Black Twisted Pine took one step toward Belcher. Longarm threw an arm out in front of the man, holding him back. Belcher and the other soldiers were all armed with Winchesters. Just then yet another soldier appeared about twenty feet up the slope from the others. He lowered a Gatling gun from his shoulder and spread the tripod it wasn't mounted on atop a flat-topped boulder. The redheaded private with a broad, freckled, sunburned face, slanted the barrel toward the canyon, eyes threatening beneath the brim of his leather-billed hat.

Belcher glanced up at the Gatling gun and then returned his maddeningly self-assured gaze back toward the canyon. "Marshal Long, War Cloud—I suggest you step aside. I am having my men arrest this man and take him back to Fort McHenry to await court-martial."

"On what charge?" Longarm asked, incredulous.

"Why, for the killing of my wife, of course." Belcher studied Longarm and then scowled with feigned incredulity. "Surely, you don't believe what he said about *my* having killed Lucy?" He gave a caustic chuff. "He somehow filled the poor girl's head with a bunch of nonsense about this mountain, convincing her to run off with him, and then, being the savage that he is, killed her. Probably got tired of her and cut her throat . . . or maybe he was drunk on *tiswin*. The Apaches love that stuff, you know."

As he'd spoke that last sentence, Belcher had turned his gaze up canyon. Longarm looked in the same direction. The other Apaches were walking toward him, all staring through the scaffolds at the soldiers, some

nocking arrows, others bringing old-model Springfield or Spencer rifles to their shoulders.

Belcher jerked a suddenly nervous gaze at War Cloud. "Keep them back! I have a Gatling gun here, and I will not hesitate in the slightest to cut them down. To cut them all down—to a man! Hell, I'd get a medal for it!"

Both War Cloud and Black Twisted Pine thrust their hands out, forestalling the dozen or so warriors. They all stopped as a loosely formed group, some dropping to their knees, all keeping their angry gazes on the soldiers.

Black Twisted Pine shouted at his people to stay back, that the soldiers were after him, not them.

Then he turned to Belcher. "You are a liar, white man. But if you promise to leave my people alone, and just take me, I will come with you willingly."

"Hold on!" Longarm stepped forward, his face flushed with fury. "Belcher, it's Black Twisted Pine I believe. Not you. And none of you other men should believe the major, either." He glanced at Captain Kilroy, who looked as though he were trying to pass a kidney stone. "What about you, Captain. You know both the major and Black Twisted Pine. Who do you believe?"

Belcher pointed angrily at Longarm. "Marshal, you're obstructing justice! One more word out of you, and I'll shoot you myself!"

He snapped his Winchester to his shoulder and aimed down the barrel, his eyes flashing wickedly.

"Major!" War Cloud shouted, taking one step forward.

Longarm grabbed the scout's arm, pulling him back.

Belcher shifted his rifle to War Cloud. To the soldier manning the Gatling gun, he said, "Private Daniels, if we do not have Black Twisted Pine in custody by the time I've counted to five, open up with your Gatling. Start with those savages just up canyon there. Take them all down, do you understand?"

Private Daniels hesitated. Then he nodded and lowered his head to aim down the Gatling gun, which he swung up canyon, toward the Chiricahuas.

Belcher looked at Longarm and quirked his lips with that menacing, jeering grin. "Marshal, stand aside. I'm taking Black Twisted Pine into custody. I do hope that he won't be shot for resisting arrest. And that I do not have to shoot you and your redskin scout for obstructing justice."

Longarm felt as though his heart would explode from the raw anger flaring behind it. He said, "You won't get away with it, Major. If you take Black Twisted Pine, you'd best make damn sure he arrives safely at McHenry, or I will personally see you hang, you son of a bitch!"

Belcher smiled down the barrel of his Winchester, which he shifted around between Longarm, War Cloud, and Black Twisted Pine.

"It is all right, lawman," Black Twisted Pine said, his voice hard and even. He started forward. "I will go with the soldiers."

In the upper periphery of his vision, Longarm saw Magpie rise up from behind a rock jutting from the side of the ridge, about fifteen feet above Private Daniels manning the Gatling gun. The girl stepped off the rock and dropped straight down, landing just behind Daniels with a grunt, bending her knees.

Daniels jerked with a start, began to swing around

toward Magpie. The girl tightened her jaws and bunched her lips as she smashed the butt of her pistol across the private's left temple.

Daniels gave a clipped scream and crumpled beside the Gatling gun.

Magpie leaped over him and hunkered down behind the gun, giving a wicked war cry, and swung the maw with a squeak of its swivel toward Belcher. The major swung around, aiming his Winchester. The rifle roared but his shot whipped over Magpie's head to slam into the ridge wall behind her.

Magpie aimed at Belcher, squinting her dark eyes over the Gatling's maw. Belcher jerked back against a boulder and out of the line of Magpie's fire.

Longarm ripped his Colt from its holster and shouted, "Hold it, Major!"

"Kill 'em!" Belcher shouted, fumbling his rifle around toward Longarm.

Longarm snapped his pistol up and fired.

At Kilroy threw his hands up, he shouted at the other soldiers, "Stand down, men! Hold your fire!"

Belcher slammed back against the boulder and, dropping his rifle, clutched his left shoulder from which blood was oozing, staining his dark blue tunic.

At the other soldiers raising their rifles tensely, Kilroy again shouted, "Stand down! Stand down!"

Belcher loosed an enraged bellow and then swung around and ran through a notch in the ridge behind him, below and right of Magpie, who tracked him with the Gatling gun, turning the crank and throwing several belching rounds at the man, all her shots merely pluming the dust at the major's heels.

Longarm shouted, "Everyone stand down!" as he bolted forward and up the face of the ridge. He glanced once at Captain Kilroy, who raised his left hand in supplication, lowering the rifle in his right hand. Longarm bolted past the soldiers and ran into the notch.

Belcher was ahead of him, running hard but sort of crouched forward, cupping his wounded shoulder. A booted foot and part of a denim-clad leg suddenly angled out from the rock wall in front of him. Belcher screamed as he tripped. He hit the ground and rolled, dust rising around him.

He lost his hat and one suspender slid off his shoulder.

He turned and rose up on his heels, his face a red mask behind his dark mustache and a generous coating of dust. His lips shone white between his teeth as he grinned savagely and extended his army-issue .44 at Leslie McPherson, who had just then stepped out from a small alcove in the ridge wall, facing him, screaming, "Why, Anson? *Whyyyy?*"

Longarm stopped running and raised his own .44. The gun leaped and roared, stabbing flames at Belcher. The bullet punched through the major's right shoulder, slamming him straight back as he triggered his revolver into the air.

He lay gasping, writhing, grinding the spurred heels of his cavalry boots into the dirt.

Longarm walked forward. He stood beside Leslie staring down at Belcher. Blue Feather walked out from behind another boulder to glare down at the man, as well.

Belcher stared up at them, fear and rage sharp and

bright in his eyes. He gritted his teeth, snarling like a wounded bobcat.

"To answer your question, girl," Longarm said, wrapping an arm around Leslie's shoulders and drawing her tight against him. "He's a coward."

War Cloud, Magpie, and Black Twisted Pine walked up behind Longarm and the two other women to stare down at Belcher. And then Kilroy and the other soldiers came, as well—all with guns lowered. The Apaches, including Stalking Puma, joined them, too, and they all stood as one group staring down at the writhing, snapping, cursing, incoherent beast that was Anson Belcher.

"Let's get him doctored," Longarm said finally, sheathing his Colt. "We want him facing the court-martial and gallows in perfect health."

Watch for

LONGARM AND THE STAR SALOON

the 422nd novel in the exciting LONGARM
series from Jove

Coming in January!

Watch for

LONGARM AND THE STAGE SALOON

the 437th novel in the exciting LONGARM
series from Jove

Coming in January!

LONGARM

GIANT-SIZED ADVENTURE FROM AVENGING ANGEL LONGARM.

BY TABOR EVANS

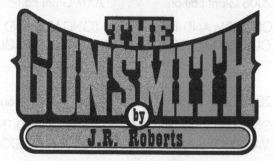